Praise for The K

"Iacovelli imbues the narrator's rants with an uncompromising precision; to him, Burberry perfume smells like 'rotten fruit tossed in a blender with noxious chemicals.' It's hard to look away from this disturbing character study"

—*Publishers Weekly*

"A profound deep dive into the human condition and unnervingly emblematic of 21st Century America, Paolo Iacovelli's stunning debut novel explores the existential despair of a gambling man. The eventual loss of all whom he loves, along with his seemingly enviable life sends him on an impossible quest to fill the void that leads to a horrific, decidedly unexpected and yet inevitable, conclusion."

—**Binnie Kirshenbaum, author of *Rabbits for Food***

"In *The King of Video Poker*, Paolo Iacovelli's nameless narrator does for today's Las Vegas strip—in other words, America—what Dostoevsky's Raskolnikov did for Tsarist Saint Petersburg or Fassbinder's Franz Biberkopf for interbellum Berlin. Unlikeable narrators are difficult to pull off and often reveal more about their environment than themselves, but Iacovelli keeps us turning the pages into a neon emptiness that is as damning as it is dark."

—**Alexander Boldizar, author of *The Man Who Saw Seconds***

"Taut and full of menace, *The King of Video Poker* captures our particular American sickness with disturbing precision and dark momentum. Paolo Iacovelli has written a very promising debut."

—**Sam Lipsyte, author of *Venus Drive* and *No One Left to Come Looking for You***

"A mesmerizing account of one man's descent into nihilism, Paolo Iacovelli's *The King of Video Poker* is unlike any novel I've read before. Iacovelli is a master of conveying the peculiarities of America, its contradictions, its desperation, and even its eerie beauty. I read this brilliant novel years ago and I still think about it all the time."

—Lauren Grodstein, author of *We Must Not Think of Ourselves*

"If you don't know what this book is about, don't look it up, just read it—it's one of the most horrifyingly effective twists I've read in years. But even if you do, *The King of Video Poker* is a masterful character study, a thorough examination of the anhedonia and banality at the root of freelance American violence. Paolo Iacovelli is compassionate, menacing, and bleakly (BLEAKLY) funny—a writer you can bet on."

—Tony Tulathimutte, author of *Private Citizens: A Novel*

"Seismic stone cold stunner debut"

—Megan Nolan, author of *Ordinary Human Failings: A Novel*

"*The King of Video Poker* delivers a new era of NY literati. Paolo Iacovelli's debut is a bold undertaking and brilliantly executed."

—Kelly Cutrone, Founder of People's Revolution, and New York Times best-selling author of *If You Have to Cry, Go Outside*

THE KING OF VIDEO POKER

PAOLO IACOVELLI

CL◀SH

Copyright © 2024 by Paolo Iacovelli
Cover by Matthew Revert
Author photo by Andrea Surget
ISBN: 9781960988089
CLASH Books
Troy, NY
clashbooks.com

To Victoria

"Existence alone had never been enough for him; he had always wanted more. Perhaps it was only from the force of his desires that he had regarded himself as a man to whom more was permitted than to others."

—*Dostoevsky, Crime and Punishment*

PART I

Arnold Palmer died today. The news anchor announces it on the TV hanging in the corner as I'm dealt a pair of 9's at a Jacks or Better machine. Suddenly it doesn't matter that the news anchor previously stated an unarmed twelve-year-old boy was shot dead by a police officer for stealing a Snickers bar. It doesn't matter that I'm a middle-aged white man who travels an hour and a half from Mesquite to Las Vegas five times a week to play high-stakes video poker and hasn't won in fourteen days. And it doesn't matter that the AC blasting on the casino floor at the Wynn doesn't cool my sweat stains from the arid desert heat outside. All that matters, even though I haven't heard his name in years, is that Arnold Palmer is dead.

"Are you okay, buddy?" the man sitting at the machine next to me asks. "You look like you're going to cry," he pauses, trying to look over at my screen. "Your hand can't be that bad."

"He died," I say.

"Who died?"

"Arnold Palmer."

"What?" the man asks, laughing.

I repeat that Arnold Palmer died and I explain how he was a trailblazer, how his humble background and plain-spoken popularity helped change the perception of golf from an elite, upper-class pastime to a more populist sport accessible to middle and working classes, how he single-handedly transcended the game of golf, took it from one level to a whole new higher level, and I keep talking about Arnold Palmer, my eyes welling with tears, mentioning that between 1960–1963 he won 29 PGA Tour events when the man interrupts me.

"That's the stupidest thing I've ever heard," he says.

I imagine cracking the screen in front of him by slamming his head into it, like hurling a bowling ball into an old TV. But my hands are trembling and then my head starts to spin and my stomach tightens. And I have to grip onto the video poker machine in order to keep myself from passing out. I manage to swallow a few Valium and then decide to go find Tim, my fifteen-year-old son, and Natalia, my second wife. I told them to come to Vegas with me today so we could spend time as a family but they haven't left the pool all day and the sun is too hot. They used to spend the weekends with me in Vegas when Tim was younger. We would ride the High Roller Ferris wheel and the Big Apple roller coaster and we'd get lunch at the Rainforest Cafe where Tim would order the fish sticks and we'd watch the volcano erupt outside the Mirage and see the hammerhead sharks and stingrays glide overhead at the Mandalay Bay aquarium. At some point, Natalia would go on a shopping spree. And I'd spend all night gambling, racking up enough points so the whole weekend would be free—everything comped, not only the valet fee.

I'm walking across the red floral carpeted casino floor toward the pool when the fire alarm goes off. The sprinklers aren't activated and I don't see any flames and I don't smell anything burning but the alarm is ringing, roaring, and the bellboys and concierges and all the employees are calmly escorting people out. The first thing that comes to mind is: someone is robbing the casino.

This is a decoy. A way to get everybody out. I think about how often casino robberies happen. The New York-New York incident: where the suspect held up the cage at gunpoint and ran off with $30,000 but got caught because he hailed a taxi. The Bellagio robbery: when a masked man stole $500,000 worth of cash and chips but was caught because he visited the casino a month earlier with the same car. The Cosmopolitan: hit three times by the Senior Pastor of the Grace Bible Church of Las Vegas who brandished a fake gun and finally got caught because it was an inside job with his wife, the shift manager. I try to think about the last casino fire but nothing comes to mind besides the infamous MGM grand fire in the '80s where over 80 people died. The odds that this is a robbery are higher.

"Everybody please calmly exit the building this way," a security guard announces. I try walking discreetly in the opposite direction, away from the crowd—if this is a robbery, somebody in the crowd will most likely be taken as a hostage or fall victim to crossfire. I hate crowds. You're like a sitting duck. I don't get very far, not even past the baccarat tables, when another security guard, some short Mexican guy, stops me.

"I'm lost," I say.

"This is not an exit," he says, before escorting me out.

Outside, casino customers and hotel guests are standing beneath palm trees on the sun-soaked sidewalk, holding as many chips as they could have grabbed off the tables. Firetrucks arrive on the scene and firefighters rush into the Wynn in their molded sponge rubber looking like the creature from the black lagoon as everybody else waits impatiently in the baking afternoon.

Howard, the casino manager, walks over to the chief firefighter. Howard is French and his real name is Jean-Jacques Apollinaire de la Guard-du-Nord but he got sick of Americans butchering it when he came to the U.S. so he changed it to Howard. He told me, one night over sushi and sake, that he picked the name after Howard Stern, even though they look nothing alike. Howard has short, curly gray hair and an elephant seal-like nose and I've never seen him wear the same suit twice.

A security guard shouts for everyone to clear the entrance. People shuffle away and some man with a ten-gallon cowboy hat drops several of his chips and another man, one with a handlebar mustache, picks them up but he doesn't hand them back and a scuffle breaks out. The security guard tries to break it up but the man with the ten-gallon cowboy hat accidentally punches the security guard and the security guard then starts pounding him to the floor. The man with the handlebar mustache joins the security guard and they team up on him, kicking him while he's down. A firefighter lights a cigarette and laughs. Howard then steps in and breaks it up. An androgynous street performer wearing red overalls, an eyepatch, and an orange mullet wig is singing, "Is there life on Mars?" but he's out of key and nobody pays attention to him. And I don't know if it's the Valium I took earlier or the still heat or the queer lyrics of this song but everything feels like that melting clock in the desert. A woman talking to her pet iguana. A hand sliding up a poinsettia-patterned skirt. Two Elvis impersonators tossing dice on the pavement. The kid of some Dutch family taking a picture with Batman and Batman aggressively telling the family to pay him his five bucks and the family trying to communicate something in broken English and Batman shouting with his fists in the air that they belong on a farm. The firefighters exit the casino with their oxygen tanks intact and announce it was a false alarm.

"Natalia is worried about you," Tim says, showing up out of nowhere, a towel wrapped around his neck, his blue bathing suit dripping.

I don't say anything, just stand there, looking out into the distance.

"Did they put out the fire?" Tim asks.

"Arnold Palmer died," I say.

I wake up, staring at the ceiling, wondering if Arnold Palmer's death was a nightmare, and reach for my phone on the nightstand to check the news. It wasn't. The digital alarm clock reads one in the afternoon. Tim is in school. Natalia is probably at her Zumba class. I think about driving to Vegas but instead sink my face into the pillow and try to fall back asleep, telling myself *this* is the nightmare. My mouth is dry and itching and the sun peering through the Venetian blinds is bright so I get up, walk over to the bathroom, and drink some cold water from the faucet. I stare at the mirror for a while, notice my bald spot and the bags under my eyes, and contemplate showering but the idea of getting wet turns me off and instead I grab a pill bottle out of the mirrored cabinet and swallow a few Valium.

Downstairs, I shut all the shades, take out an old slice of pepperoni pizza from the fridge, heat it up in the microwave, sit on the couch in my boxers, and eat it while staring at the black television screen. I feel the tomato sauce drip down my chin but I can't get myself to stand up and grab a napkin from the kitchen so I just wipe my chin with my white T-shirt.

I drive to the strip mall in Mesquite and sit in the parking lot for a while, the heat from the sun warming the inside of the car, watching families unload big plastic bags off shopping carts, into their Buicks or Kias or Honda Civics, and then I walk into Target and the cool air conditioned store relaxes me and I try to buy a Coke but realize they only sell eight packs and I only want one so I leave empty-handed and wander aimlessly around the strip mall and then I find myself in a Jamba Juice and ask for an Arnold Palmer but the man behind the cash register informs me they don't make that and then he asks if I'm okay and I tell him I'm just tired and order a Strawberries Gone Bananas instead and then in the parking lot I give it to a shirtless bum muttering how we're all going to die from this heat wave and then I sit in my car and I notice the thermometer reads 104 degrees and blast the AC and look up the weather in other places around the world and it's 74 degrees in Coronado and 80 degrees in Tahiti and 76 degrees in Cape Town and I stare at the palm trees shifting in the warm desert wind until some teenagers in an idling BMW honk at me for my spot and call me an asshole.

I drive to the supermarket to buy some iced tea and lemonade so I can make myself an Arnold Palmer but I can't find the beverage section. I keep circling the same two aisles for what feels like an eternity until I end up getting lost and find myself back at the entrance. And I realize they now have a self-service checkout and this quells some of my anxiety because I won't have to engage in meaningless small talk with the loafer cashier and I won't have to lie when she asks in the most perfunctory manner "How are *you* doing today?" I walk up to the nearest stock clerk, a middle-aged woman with yellowing teeth, gray hair, and dirt stuck underneath her unpolished nails, the type of person who looks like she'd kill me if I had any opioids in my pocket, and I ask her where the beverage section is. She tells me aisle 18. There are 13 different lemonades; 15 different iced teas. There's even an Arizona already-made Arnold Palmer that's a half-and-half version.

I remember one summer when I was ten, or maybe twelve, at Laguna Beach, my father introduced me to the drink, explained how it's a common misconception that it's half and half, how it's technically supposed to be two parts lemonade, one part iced tea. I remember thinking he seemed happy that day, his short, blond hair blowing in the wind, singing along to Sam Cooke's "A Change Is Gonna Come," which blared out of our beat-up radio, as he danced with my mother under a Californian sun.

"Excuse me," a man says, walking past me. I'm still standing in this massive supermarket, staring at an endless wall of non-alcoholic beverages, and I can't decide which one to pick and my vision becomes blurry, to the point where I can no longer even tell the lemonades and iced teas apart. All I see is the glowing image of my father slow-dancing with my mother on that shimmering beach, and my eyes water up and for some reason, the supermarket feels like too much. I leave.

$\mathbf{M}$y father was born in Sheboygan, Wisconsin in 1926. He attended high school in Chicago and served in the Navy as an S2 (Seaman Second Class) during World War II. He used to tell me stories about the trouble he would get into abroad, the group of kids in Italy who tried to mug him, how he bamboozled some of his peers to carry out his loose cigarette scheme, the way he'd seduce women without speaking their native tongue. He had a large presence. He was big-boned by nature, stood 6 feet and 4 inches tall, and weighed roughly 245 pounds. He was also silver-tongued and had a way of charming everyone. Everybody in the neighborhood loved him, and any room he entered had a strange way of orbiting around him. He could have convinced the mailman to run off with him. My mother told me they met at a party in Chicago where they danced the night away to Duke Ellington as my father played boogie-woogie banjo and told her all his big plans. They got married in Reno in 1952 and spent the next few years bouncing around the country until they decided to settle down in the San Fernando Valley.

He always wore violet-tinted glasses but underneath them, his green eyes would be as alert as a serpent's. He had blond hair but was balding and was rather sensitive about the issue. When his friends would come over they

called him "Chromedome." He had a scar above his right
eyebrow and on his right knee from his Navy days and he
had a birthmark on his left ankle the shape of a flamingo.
He smoked Camel cigarettes and Dutch Masters cigars.
He liked hot rods, sports, gambling, and steak, and always
drank room-temperature water, joking that cold water was
bad for his singing voice. He was an avid bridge player. He
talked about wanting to start a church in Las Vegas. He
worked as an auto mechanic, electrician, promoter, sales-
man, caddie, service station attendant, and a nightclub
operator. The nightclub was called "Big Daddy's." He was
Big Daddy.

During his spare time, he volunteered for the local
search-and-rescue team and counseled wayward kids, mentioning he wanted to use the mistakes he had made in his
troubled youth to help youngsters stay "on the straight and
narrow." He carried a snub-nosed revolver in his underwear
that he called his "second gun" and he drove a cream-colored
Pontiac station wagon. He used to tell fanciful stories about
his past, claiming he'd been a Dixieland band singer, a pilot,
an auto racing crew chief, a Chicago Bears pro football player, a survivor of a World War II minesweeper sinking, and a
famous wrestler named "Crybaby." He also operated a bingo
parlor where he ran an underground poker ring. He used to
call J. Edgar Hoover a "Grade A pansy."

Entering my house, I walk straight to the kitchen, grab a half-empty bottle of whiskey above the fridge and take a sip. Natalia is sitting on the couch with Tim, and when I ask her why Tim isn't in school she informs me that today is Sunday and I just nod and make my way to the backyard, clutching the bottle. I sit on a chaise longue, gazing at my house, which is a lot nicer than my neighbors'.

I bought it two years ago for less than half the market price. The real estate agent disclosed that the previous owners, a family of five, were brutally murdered in the house one night. The Nevada coroner's office reported that each victim had been stabbed repeatedly. The police never found the suspect or even got close to a motive. The whole thing seemed like a random act of violence; besides a bag of bloody clothes, a knife, and a towel that read "pig," which were uncovered in the hills, all they found were the five bodies with slit throats floating face down in the pool. Because nobody else wanted to live in a "cursed" house and because nobody else realized that if the previous owners had a gun tucked away in the nightstand they would have survived (I have two gun lockers, one in my study and the other in the garage), I was able to capitalize on the deal of a lifetime and purchased this 2,500 square foot house with a pool, three bedrooms, three bathrooms, and granite countertops for 150k in cash. I never told Natalia because she already has nightmares and doesn't need them entertained.

The American flag hanging above the glass doors looks faded and I tell myself I need a new one. Natalia then sits down on the chair beside me and asks if I ended up having any luck last night and I don't say anything, just stare at the palm tree shivering in the warm wind. She starts telling me how she can remove the bandages today, urges me to check it out for myself—she's talking about her breast implants, which she's wanted for a while and I finally agreed to pay for—but I block her out, focus on a bee drowning in the pool, shriveling. She nudges my arm, asking, "Are you okay?"

I'm at the dinner table, eating pasta with cherry tomatoes and zucchini, which Natalia cooked, and nobody is saying anything so I decide to break the silence and ask Tim how school is going.

"Fine," he says, staring at his plate, watching a penne slide off a fork prong.

"How's George?" I ask.

"What?"

"George. How's he doing?"

"George Andrews? I haven't hung out with him since I was thirteen."

"Oh," I pause, "not George then, that other kid."

"Zack?"

"Yeah, Zack," I say. "How's Zack?"

Tim asks if I can pass the water pitcher and I pour him a glass but my mind drifts and suddenly I'm over-pouring, water overflowing, and Natalia gets up and grabs a handful of napkins.

In the bedroom, Natalia slips out of her black nightgown, takes my hand, and places it on her new breast, smiling. I cup her balloon-like breast. Natalia then gives me a lewd glance, pushes me onto the bed, and goes down on me, but I don't get hard, and after a while, she brings her head up and asks what's wrong. "Nothing," I say, "I'm just tired." She stares at me for a long second, annoyed, and then turns off the lights.

I met Natalia at a casino in Reno two years after my wife died. She was the hostess. I cracked a joke, "How do you make Holy water? You boil the hell out of it." She laughed. We went out on a few dates. I wasn't sure if I loved her or not, but she was really good with Tim, who was twelve at the time, so I asked her to quit her job and move in with me. Two months later we got married at the Graceland Chapel in Las Vegas, where we rented a pink Cadillac and were legally wed by an Elvis impersonator who sang "Can't Help Falling in Love." Now, when she isn't taking care of Tim, she works at a suicide hotline a couple days a week, but I think that's just to give her life meaning, it makes her feel special.

I'm lying in bed, awake, staring at the ceiling, listening to the trees rustling in the wind and the hum of the fan, wondering if someone will be as distraught over the announcement of my death, but the coyotes howling in the distance seem to answer my question. I keep tossing and turning all night, restless, unable to sleep, my mind wandering to places it hasn't gone in a while. *I'm dragging Lucy across the street, over to the dry, uncut grass in our backyard, the faint sound of the ice cream truck's jingle blaring. I stare down at Lucy who's lying in my arms, comatose, blood staining my hands. My father comes out of the back door, wearing his black work boots covered in grime and soot, ripped jeans, a white T-shirt, and shouts out, "Dinner is ready" but I don't answer, I don't even look up, my gaze on Lucy. My father staggers over, telling me my brothers are already at the table. "Why won't she wake up?" I ask. My father then sees the blood on my hands and the dog's lifeless eyes. "What happened?" my father asks, in shock, "What did you do?" He picks up the dog, hugging her tightly, his green eyes tearing, his sobs muffled in her white fur. I try to say something but nothing comes out. "You killed her?" my father says loudly. "It wasn't me, it was the truck," I mumble, licking my lips, the taste of pennies in my mouth. My father gently places the dog on the grass, wipes the tear streaming down his cheek, and then stands up. He looks into my eyes and slaps me across the face with the back of his hand, hard, his golden ring cutting me. "Do you see what you've done?" my father shouts, "You're a goddamn monster!" My father hits me again, harder this time, and he keeps hitting me, harder and harder, as if in a boxing ring, the bell never ringing.*

"Hey," I say, shaking Natalia, trying to wake her up. "Are you awake?"

"I am now," she says, rolling over to face me.

"Does…" my voice trails off. "Does Tim hate me?"

Coyotes howl in the distance.

It has to do with the scallops. The reason I'm a regular at the Wynn over all the other casinos in Vegas. It has nothing to do with the fact that the Bellagio stopped comping everything after they realized my winning streak was based on talent and not sheer luck. Nor does it have to do with the fact that I lost a slip-and-fall lawsuit against the Cosmopolitan. It has to do with the scallops at the Wynn's all-day buffet, which features 15 live-action cooking stations with rotisserie grilled steakhouse cuts, coast-to-coast seafood, and more than 120 artfully presented dishes. The lavish spread includes every kind of food imaginable. If you can think it, they have it. Some of the more refined items on the menu: double-cut lamb chops with truffle spinach and crispy onions, lobster-stuffed ravioli with roasted red peppers, fennel and a saffron sauce, steak and lobster topped with a Bearnaise sauce. But the Old Bay-braised scallops served with a spicy tomato compote steal the show.

I usually beat the buffet, then play video poker for hours late into the night. When I take a bite from one of the scallops today it tastes mealy and I wonder if they changed distributor. I don't finish them and I don't eat anything else. Instead I watch a woman stuff mozzarella sticks down her pants before I decide to walk across the casino floor, past someone who could be Celine Dion eating a cheeseburger, over to the high-stakes video poker area.

I sit down at my Jacks or Better machine. The machine I've deemed mine is in the corner, away from people, and next to an emergency exit, in case something bad were to happen. I have also tried out the chairs of the other machines not unlike at a mattress store, and even though this chair is at the end of a row of brown identical-looking chairs, this one is unique, the best. The plumpness of the cold-cured foam gives a high resilience and the state-of-the-art ergonomic design ensures comfort for hours on end and I have sat in it to such length that it has been molded perfectly to my weight and size. I find it more comfortable than the chairs in my house in Mesquite.

I slide in my Loyalty Reward card, set the bet to $100, and hit the deal button. I'm dealt: K of spades, 3 of diamonds, J of diamonds, 5 of spades, and 8 of spades. I hold the three spades. I hit the draw button, hoping for two more spades. I'm dealt: 4 of heart, and 4 of diamonds. Not even close. Game Over.

I readjust in the chair, hit the deal button again. I'm dealt: K of diamonds, 10 of hearts, 4 of clubs, J of clubs, 9 of diamonds. I hold the K of diamonds and the J of clubs. I hit the draw button, hoping for a pair of K or J. I'm dealt: A of hearts, 9 of spades, 4 of diamonds. Game Over.

I hit the deal button again. I'm dealt: 5 of diamonds, 8 of hearts, 9 of hearts, J of diamonds, 2 of hearts. I hold the 8, 9, and 2 of hearts. I hit the draw button, hoping for two hearts. I'm dealt: A of hearts, 2 of diamonds. Off by one. Game Over.

I rub my temples, take a deep breath, and go again.

"Why don't you just go to the River today?" Natalia asks, referring to a local casino in Mesquite, as I'm heading out the door.

"Because," I clear my throat. "This big fish needs an ocean, not a river."

Natalia rolls her eyes.

Driving to Vegas, the hot wind blowing orange dust through the windows, the sun warm against my face, I think back to when I was fifteen and growing up under the freeway in the San Fernando Valley. I remember the time our neighbor, Miss Mooney, brought me to the pool at a motel she worked at several blocks away because of a misunderstanding with the police, the smell of chlorine and cheap sunblock and the hot Pepsi she got me from the vending machine and the worried expression on her face when she offered to play Marco Polo, which I thought was because I wasn't a good swimmer. I try not to think about what happened after, when she dropped me back home. Instead I wonder whether the towels from the motel were red with white stripes or white with red stripes. I miss the exit for Vegas and keep driving, until I no longer smell the chlorine, until I no longer see the worried expression on Miss Mooney's face, until the palm trees start to swoosh by rhythmically. It isn't until I reach the Grand Canyon that I remember there were no stripes on the towels. That night the AC is busted in the bedroom and the heat keeps me up and I try sleeping out by the pool but the air is hot and arid and I end up sitting on the couch, swallowing a few Valium, watching old PGA tours on TV. At least there's Arnold Palmer.

Driving from Mesquite to Vegas, I turn up the radio. On the Las Vegas Daily news station: missing girls visiting from Kansas City found decapitated in the Mojave desert, four Asians dead in a massage parlor shooting, the plans for a new megacasino being built by MGM where the Stardust stood. I have driven down this freeway so many times it's become muscle memory, I could close my eyes and open them an hour and a half later and be on the Strip, pulling up to the Wynn. It's like I know every tumbleweed by its name. Soaring vultures land on a billboard ahead, the one that marks the midway point between Mesquite to Vegas. And I can't make out the billboard in the hazy heat from this distance but from what I can see the blurred colors are no longer blue and gold. For as long as I remember it has been an ad for the Bellagio, a picture of the fountains erupting before the brightly-lit resort. It hasn't come to mean anything more to me besides being a point of reference, the fountains letting me know that I'm halfway there, and it's usually around the time the dread shifts into mild excitement. As I approach the billboard, I slow down and look at it. It's now white and all it says is "No Limits" in huge black Helvetica letters and even though it's probably an ad for some other casino, the lack of context unsettles me and I step on the gas hard and try not to think about it and when I reach the last stretch of the drive where the road dips, displaying the neon lights in the sun-baked valley below, I get this strange sensation that somebody else is driving my car, that I am watching myself steer from an aerial view. It isn't until I'm sitting at my video poker machine at the Wynn that I stop thinking about the billboard.

After handing my keys to the valet and after walking into the Wynn wearing sandals and sweatpants and a stained T-shirt and after a man with dress shoes so black they gleam purple approaches and tells me panhandlers aren't allowed

in here and after Howard, the casino manager with an elephant seal nose, informs him I'm a regular, I'm escorted past
the slot machines and the blackjack tables and poker tables
and craps, over to my high-stakes video poker machine.
Howard tells me he's comping the presidential suite for me
tonight before walking away. I nod since everything is always
comped anyway. I slide in my Loyalty Reward card, which
has a $100,000 credit limit, ready to place my first $100 bet.
But from where I'm sitting I can see the cocktail waitresses
and the overdressed bachelors and the old women with di-
abetes holding cups of pennies all going about their lives,
letting the chips fall where they may, and I realize nobody
cares about Arnold Palmer dying and I can't get myself to
place my first bet. I watch a high-roller tip a cocktail waitress
to get shoes for him to try on from the Gucci store across
the casino while he plays poker. I think about the billboard
that says, "No Limits."

Then I go to the bathroom, splash water on my face, and
lock myself in a stall. I call Natalia but she doesn't answer.
After twenty minutes or so, I decide to get a drink at the hotel
bar, where an Elvis impersonator ends up telling me he lost
his family due to his crippling meth addiction and has been
sober for a year. Natalia calls me back but I don't answer. A
couple at a table raises their glass and toasts to something. The
man, who is wearing a red bowtie, kisses her hand. I down
my whiskey and suddenly *I'm at the West Shore Country Club
on a Friday afternoon, after school, with my father.* "Y'know,

son, my job is the most important job on a golf course. No matter how good the golfer, without a good caddie, he'd be absolutely nowhere. A caddie has to have an exceptional awareness of the game in order to calculate every move, anticipate the challenges and obstacles of the course and have a keen awareness of the best strategy in order to win. It requires a very specific kind of intelligence and not many people can do it."

"Why not just be a golfer then?" I ask. My father looks at me and, raising his voice, says, "Because being a caddie is harder!" I nod. "Who am I kidding?" my father says after a while, taking a deep breath, "All I do is carry people's bags and clubs. I give them my first-rate advice, first rate advice, but they never heed it. Of course not, right? That would require them to think that I'm not just the ball boy. Maybe I should become a golfer, you're right, I could positively do it." His initial air of confidence fades and a hint of doubt appears on his face. "No, I'm sure I could. It would just take some time before I actually made any money from it and I don't want to do that to your mother," his voice trails off. "Yeah that's it," he says, wagging his forefinger, having found the reason, "I could do it, it would just be hard on your mother." My father looks out into the horizon, where the soft pink sky meets the field of bright grass, lost in thought.

"Can we go, dad?" I ask. "C'mon, let's go work on your backswing," he says. On our way to the practice range, we come across a clamorous crowd of people, of envious-looking men and drop-dead gorgeous women, shouting for autographs, snapping pictures, circling a handsome man wearing an open three-button

Munsingwear polo tucked in his trousers; he has a tan complexion, short brown hair, soft hazel eyes, and a cigarette in his mouth, and he strolls nonchalantly past them all, smiling, emitting an aura of boyish charm and rugged masculinity. as they kiss his hands. "That's the King!" my father exclaims, starstruck, "music has Elvis, golf has Arnold Palmer." I look at this figure, thinking I want a crowd of people to kiss my hands when I grow up. "You know he learned how to play golf from his father? He was a grounds-keep," my father says proudly. "That could be you one day, son. He's an American hero. Just remember, wanting it isn't enough, you have to sacrifice everything."

I'm at the valet stand picking up my car when I notice a dent in the bumper. I remember my father telling me about the time Arnold Palmer stopped an entire PGA Tour in Palm Springs because someone stole his lucky head-heavy club. He didn't resume playing until it was returned to him and even though it turned out only to be a fan, it was the principle, my father had explained. The valet, some Mexican guy, tries to hand me the keys. I don't take them.

"What happened?" I point to the bumper.

"What do you mean?" the valet asks.

"There's a dent."

"I don't see anything."

"I want to know what happened to my car."

"Nothing happened, sir."

I look around, count how many people are waiting in line. "Listen, it's very simple. Nobody is getting their car back until you tell me where this dent came from."

"I don't see a dent, sir," he says. "Maybe it was already there."

"If it was already there does that mean you admit you see a dent?"

The valet doesn't say anything.

Howard ends up coming over, and the valet tenses up when he notices the way Howard greets me like we're old college buddies, and Howard asks me what's wrong.

"I'll get it fixed for you," Howard says, readjusting his pink tie.

"I don't want it fixed."

"Do you want a new car?" Howard asks. "I can get you that. No problem."

"No."

"Did you see that beautiful Porsche in the lobby? That can be yours. Would be a nice upgrade from that old Honda of yours, wouldn't it?"

"I don't want a new car."

"Then what do you want?"

"I don't want to see him around here again."

"Who?" Howard asks.

"The valet."

"Effran?" Howard asks, shocked. "He's a hard worker,

I've never had any," his voice trails off. Howard glances over at the valet, then looks back at me. "Done," he pauses, takes my keys from the valet, hands them to me. "I'll make sure you never see him at the Wynn again."

"Not just the Wynn," I say, staring at the valet, who now looks like he's finally understanding the severity of what he's done and *who* he's done it to.

"You sure you don't just want a new car?" Howard asks.

"I don't want to see him at any other casino on the Strip."

"He wouldn't be able to—"

"Or you won't see me here again," I interrupt.

Down the driveway, onto Las Vegas Boulevard, I tell myself I won't get the dent fixed, a reminder to the other valets of who they're dealing with. As I pass by a shirtless bum urinating on the sidewalk, I picture the Mexican valet on the Strip with a fake leather briefcase, handing out his resume to every casino along the way and thinking about me as he gets rejected each time. For a moment I consider the odds I ruined his career, or even his life, but I quickly remember that doesn't matter. It's the principle. It's what Arnold Palmer would have done. When I get on the freeway, I think about going to the funeral but they're having it in Pennsylvania and that's too far. At some point I tell myself I could drive to Palm Springs instead and lay flowers on the 18th hole at the Bob Hope Desert Classic, the famous hole where in 1973 he beat his rival Jack Nicklaus; he had 7 feet for birdie, needed only par, sank the birdie putt, won by two, and flung his visor into the air in celebration. His final PGA Tour win.

I drive to a Taco Bell in Mesquite but there are only Mexicans inside so I decide to use the drive-thru instead and I casually order a Cheesy Gordita Crunch and a large Baja Blast and eat it in the empty parking lot and then I'm craving a glass of milk and I call the house phone to ask Natalia or Tim if we have any left but nobody answers and then I call Natalia's cell but she doesn't answer that either so I try the suicide hotline she works at and I ask for Natalia and I'm redirected to her line and when I tell her it's me she doesn't say anything for a moment and then she sounds embarrassed and whispers that she's currently talking to someone who is threatening to throw themselves in front of traffic and I say how shitty of them to put that on someone else and then I ask Natalia if we have any milk at home and Natalia hangs up and I'm left alone in my car wondering how lonely the first person to yank on an udder until white liquid expelled out and drank it must have been and then I think about how cow farts release methane and I ask myself if I could cut milk out of my diet and on my way home I think about how my mother used to buy powdered milk because she couldn't afford regular milk and I end up stopping at the supermarket and answer my question by buying five gallons.

I bring Tim to a florist shop in Mesquite. Angels Dream has the freshest flowers in all of Nevada. Howard told me they get the Wynn's flower arrangement here. Outside the shop expensive sports cars are parked, Aston Martins, Lamborghinis, Ferraris, Mustangs, and there are only two other people inside besides the florist, which makes me wonder if the owner of a flower shop can really make that much. An image enters my mind: Arnold Palmer's red Cadillac.

I take a deep inhale. "Doesn't that smell good?"

"Why are we here?" Tim asks, seeming annoyed.

I haven't asked Tim yet but I'm hoping Tim will want to come with me to Palm Springs. A father and son road trip. "To buy flowers for Arnold Palmer."

"Why?" Tim asks.

I don't answer Tim; I scan the shelves looking for red flowers and all the red flowers at the front are roses and I count 13 different species but roses are for lovers so I move toward the back to find another red flower that won't come across as quite as gay.

"How can I help you two today?" the florist asks as he shuffles over. He looks like he could be the owner and I'm tempted to ask what the deal is with all the nice cars parked outside, if he launders money.

"We're looking for the nicest bouquet of red flowers you have," I say. "It's for a very special occasion. I want nothing but the best."

"Very well," the florist says. "I have a lovely bouquet of French roses over here."

"No roses," I state.

"Uh okay," the florist says, thrown off by my standoffish response to roses. "We have plenty of other lovely red flowers. We have lovely red marigolds, lilies, chrysanthemums, cockscombs, daisies...Right this way." He motions us to follow him.

"Because a King deserves to be commemorated," I whisper to Tim as we follow the florist toward the back.

"What's the special occasion?" the florist asks, showing me a wall of red flowers, hundreds of different kinds, no roses. "If you don't mind my asking."

"Arnold Palmer's vigil," I say. But the florist doesn't say anything so I add: "Driving to Palm Springs to pay my respects."

The florist and Tim share a look, as if they both seem not to quite understand. But the florist doesn't press any further, he nods and tells me to let him know if I have any questions before walking away.

"Which ones do you prefer?" I show Tim two different bouquets.

"They look the same."

"These are red marigolds," I raise one hand. "And these," I raise the other, "are red lilies."

"What about those?" Tim points to an ugly basic bouquet in the corner.

"The Chrysanthemums?"

"Yeah sure, whatever they are."

"That's a poor man's flower," I say dismissively. "That would be an insult." Tim hands me a bouquet of red daisies but the petals are shriveled, some ripped, curling in on themselves. "He would hate these."

"Who cares?" Tim says. "He's dead. Does it matter?"

I ignore his irreverence because I don't want to get in a fight with Tim, not here. After a while of smelling all the bright red flowers, I pick out a beautiful bouquet of red marigolds and bring the petals up to my nose. "These are perfect."

"Perfect," Tim says, losing his patience.

As we wait in line, I finally ask Tim, "Why don't you come with me?"

"To Palm Springs?" Tim asks.

"Yeah."

"Why would I go to Palm Springs," Tim says.

"It could be fun?" I say, but it comes out as a question.

"I don't know," Tim says, scratching his arm.

At the cash register, the florist informs me the shelf life of these flowers once in a vase is normally around a week but because these are so fresh, if you take them out of the vase and replenish the water every two days these flowers will last a little over two weeks. All I hear is that I have at the most two weeks to convince Tim to come with me to Palm Springs. The odds look good.

"We can stop at the alien museum on our way to Palm Springs," I say in the car.

"I can't," Tim says, staring straight at the road ahead. "I have my championship game."

"I didn't even say when."

Silence.

"Well I can't this weekend," Tim says.

"We could go tomorrow."

"I have, um, school," Tim says, unsure. "I can't just miss school."

"You know my father used to tell me the ends justify the means," I say, glancing over at Tim, but the words don't seem to register with him. "When I was around your age we had this assignment in school to build a bridge and we were only supposed to use a limited amount of wood that came in the kit they gave us but I used more wood and I had the best bridge." I pause. "But it didn't matter. The ends justified the means."

Tim doesn't say anything.

"What about next weekend?" I ask after a while, at a stop sign.

"I have the state qualifiers next weekend."

Tim's phone vibrates. He checks it and smiles. I wonder if it's a girl but I don't ask. I don't say anything for the rest of the ride and when we get home I cut the ends of the red marigolds and put them in a vase in my study.

The next day, I drive to Mesquite Valley High, pull into the parking lot, put on my sunglasses, and roll down the window. I hear the bell ring and within seconds teenagers rush out the doors, swarming across the lawn, and I'm tapping my hand against the steering wheel, scanning the crowd for Tim, waiting for him to be pleasantly surprised and smile as he notices the afternoon sun glaring off my cherry-red Honda. But Tim doesn't show up and the kids empty out and I wonder if Tim is stuck in detention or smoking a joint in the bathroom or making out with a cheerleader under the bleachers. After a while, I call Natalia and ask if she knows why Tim hasn't gotten out of school yet. She tells me he has soccer practice today. I thought that was only on Monday. No, she informs me, it's on Monday, *Wednesday*, and Friday.

I hang up and drive to the soccer field and spot Tim. His blond hair is tied back and he's wearing a yellow pinny, the muscles in his calves straining as he sprints up and down the field. And I watch him from the car, surprised by how graceful of an athlete he is, at how he tackles players without a shred of doubt, at how effortlessly he outruns the defenders, at how comfortably he moves around. When practice is over, Tim's friend slaps his ass and Tim whispers something in his ear and they both laugh.

I get out of the car and shout Tim's name, but Tim doesn't smile when he sees me; instead he runs over, asking what I'm doing here. I tell him I'm here to pick him up but he doesn't say anything, just stands in front of me with his blank green eyes, clutching a sports bag, sweat dripping down his forehead. I ask him if he wants to go to Palm Springs now and he asks why and I shrug and there's a long silence and Tim says he has a ride and then I'm standing alone on the asphalt and I take off my sunglasses, watching the silver car Tim entered glide away, and then I get back in my car and drive an hour and a half to Vegas.

Howard and I are eating sushi and drinking sake at Mizuya at the Wynn later that night. I couldn't sleep and Howard was clocking out of his shift. So here we are, two men eating raw fish together, in the wee hours of the morning. He ordered a spicy salmon roll, a dragon roll, an Alaska roll, an eel roll, and a tiger roll. I told the waiter I'd have the same. "Don't worry it's just a bad luck streak," Howard says, pouring me a glass of sake.

"Good for you though," I say, raising the glass to my lips. "I've just been distracted."

"Still thinking about that golfer?" he asks.

"Yeah," I tell him.

"What a loss," Howard says. "I'd feel the same if Cantona died."

I pretend to know who that is and mention I'm trying to convince Tim to accompany me to Palm Springs.

"Must be nice to have a son." He puts wasabi in his soy sauce. "You have to bring him to Chico's, they have the fluffiest pancakes."

"What do you mean?" I ask, finishing my spicy salmon roll.

"The secret is that they separate and beat the egg whites."

"I mean about having a son."

"Oh just that it must be nice to have someone to leave everything behind for." He takes a sip of sake.

"It's not all it's made out to be," I say, after a while. "It's honestly just an excuse not to kill yourself."

"Nonsense," Howard says. "Tim is a great kid."

"He's a brat."

"Don't push too hard," Howard says. "Go to one of his soccer games and he'll come to you." He pours us another round of sake. "And if that doesn't work you could always give him a good smack across the head," he says in a tone that I can't make out whether or not he is joking. "That always worked with me when I was a kid."

"I don't know if that worked with me," I say. "But things were different back then."

"French parents hit their kids all the time. And we turn out fine."

"Then what the fuck are you doing here?" I ask.

"Land of opportunity," he says with a smirk before downing his sake.

"Did you change distributor for the buffet scallops?" I ask.

"No, why?" Howard asks

"They tasted different," I say.

"I have to piss."

"You mean you have to urinate?" I ask.

"Yeah."

"Urinate? And if your tits were bigger you'd be a ten," I say.

Howard laughs.

The waiter drops the check off at the table next to us and one of the guys says, "Do you have the memory of a goldfish or are you just plain retarded? I told you to cancel the California roll."

"Take it easy," Howard tells them.

The guy looks taken aback. "Oh yeah? Or what?"

"Or I'll have you kicked out of here."

"I'd like to see you try," the guy says, not realizing the power Howard holds.

Howard gets up from our table and stands a few inches away from the two guys and it looks like a fight is going to break out and I ask myself if I would get involved as I stare at the samurai sword on the wall. Howard whispers something in the guy's ear and the expression on his face shifts abruptly; he throws money on the table before walking away with his buddy. The waiter thanks Howard.

Howard pats him on the back and then goes to the bathroom and when he comes back he talks about how excited he is to try out a new jacuzzi he had installed in his backyard, with 24 jets, and we keep drinking sake until we're both three sheets to the wind and at some point he mumbles that he has to go home, and then I find myself sitting at a video poker machine playing through the night and I wonder if I would feel better if I installed a jacuzzi in my backyard and then I think about the mechanical aspects of the 24 jets and I imagine the pressurized streams hitting against Howard's bare back, his muscles straining, and because there are no windows or clocks in the casino it isn't until I check my phone that I realize it's six A.M. and an old lady sitting at the machine next to me is counting days and turning a chip in her hand that doesn't look like a casino chip and I wonder if she knows she's supposed to be counting cards instead and then I go to my room upstairs where nobody counts days and the lights are dark and I lie down for a few hours.

On Thursday I receive a text from my brother informing me there was a hurricane in Naples. The retirement home where our mother is staying was hit, palm trees splitting against the roof, red shingles falling to the floor. He reassures me she's fine but that she lost her walker. I make a joke my brother doesn't find funny, about how it's too bad she wasn't outside, she would have been blown away in the wind. My brother informs me of this as I check out of the Wynn and I think about my mother, her skin yellow, her head bald, withering away in an empty apartment overlooking some crocodile-infested swamp. I keep thinking about her as I make a right on the Strip and pull into a Mobil station and fill up the tank. I try to remember the last time I visited her but come up blank. I consider driving down to Florida and spending some time with her before she dies. I have no cell service so I call her from a phone booth in the gas station.

"Who is this?" she answers, sounding worse than the last time I spoke to her.

"How are you?" I ask.

"Who is this?" she asks. "Is this Eric?"

"It's your other son," I say. "Your most boring son."

She doesn't say anything.

"How are you?" I shout.

"Will you come over for Thanksgiving this year?" she shouts back. "I want to see Tim." She pauses. "I can make those marshmallow sweet potatoes you boys like and we can get eggnog and…" She stops. "Oh do you remember that Thanksgiving your father accidentally bought a chicken instead?" She laughs. "That was a good day."

I remember that Thanksgiving, going to the store with my father who purposefully bought chicken instead because it was cheaper, watching *A Charlie Brown Thanksgiving* on TV with my brothers after dinner, getting a stomach ache from drinking too much eggnog and my mother making me mint tea. I remember my father getting drunk and telling my mother he hated her. But the detail I remember more than anything, the detail that unsettles me, is that it was our last Thanksgiving as a family.

"Why did he…" I pause, noticing my hand shaking. "Why did he… " I try again but I can't finish the sentence and the call ends and I don't have any more quarters and I stand in the phone booth for a while, trying to get my hand to stop shaking.

I walk back to my car and sit in the gas station, the engine idling, watching a bum stagger barefoot across the hot asphalt, counting quarters and nickels and dimes, before entering the convenience store. He walks out chewing a piece of jerky. Instead of driving over 2,000 miles to Florida, I order a walker to my mother's address in Naples and drive back to Mesquite.

When I arrive back home, I make sure to change the water for the red marigolds. I then go to Tim's room and I look at him, this fifteen-year-old kid on his laptop, wearing a headset, playing some game, and I'm wondering why he isn't out with his friends or hanging out with a girl. And then I tell myself: I need to bond with him in order for him to want to come to Palm Springs.

"Shit," he says, "you scared me."

"Hi."

"Um, hi," he says, taking off his headset.

"What are you doing?" I ask.

"Just watching YouTube videos," he says, on edge.

"What are you watching?" I ask, trying to make conversation, even though I don't care.

"COD videos."

"What about cod fish?"

"Call of Duty. Black Ops III." He points to the screen, and then with excitement goes into it: "It takes place in 2065, 40 years after the events of the second, in a world facing upheaval from climate change and new technologies. And a new breed of Black Ops soldiers emerges and the lines are blurred between our own humanity and the cutting-edge military robotics that define the future of and," he catches himself getting overly excited, pauses, and then adds with a calm, neutral voice, "combat." He scratches the back of his neck, mumbles, "Yeah, combat."

"I see," I say, not recognizing his voice. I look around his room, at the posters of unfamiliar people and things hanging from the walls, trying to find a clue, some indication of what I can say that will engage him, but I come up blank and realize I don't really know who he is anymore. "Since when do you like Bruce Springsteen?" I ask, noticing a *Born To Run* album cover poster above his head.

"That was Mom's," he says.

"Oh." I look him straight in his blank eyes, and open my mouth, wanting to tell him I love him, but I don't know how and the words don't come out and all I end up saying is, "Okay."

Silence.

"Do you want to, um," I pause. "Go to the movies?"

"I'm sort of in the middle of something."

"Oh, yeah, sure."

He puts his headset back on.

I look at his blond hair and broad shoulders and when I close my eyes I pretend that when I open them, Tim and I will be in the backyard throwing a football, and he'll ask me for advice about some girl he has a crush on, and I'll tell him something wise and then I'll crack a joke and Tim will laugh, and we'll have the type of heartfelt father-son bonding moment you see in movies, but that doesn't happen in real life. I open my eyes. Tim has his back turned to me, staring at his computer screen. I walk out.

Later that day, I'm at the mall on Mesquite Boulevard with Tim since I lured him into spending time with me by taking him to GameStop. But before, I bring him into a Sporting Goods store and show him some golf clubs, hoping he'll want to buy a set, and he nods politely but doesn't seem interested. "Someone has to be the next Arnold Palmer," I say. But he staggers over to the soccer section, taking a jersey off the rack, gazing at it in wonder, as if he were James W.

Marshall staring at the first findings of gold in the tailrace of a lumber mill back in 1848. When I walk over to him, he asks if we can buy it, and I say, "C'mon, you don't want to be a foot fairy." I put the jersey back on the rack.

On our way out, I notice a Ralph Lauren outlet and bring Tim, thinking he could use some nice polos. I ask him if he sees anything he likes but he just shrugs, so I pick out several polos for him to try on—the Iconic Mesh Polo in Newport Navy and in Heritage Royal, the Big Pony Mesh Polo in American White and in Steel Heather. He reluctantly goes to the dressing room and tries them on, seeming unfazed by the timeless design and luxury fabric of the shirts. I try educating him on what makes them so special. I inform him that Ralph Lauren was originally named Ralph Lifshitz from Jewish immigrants but reinvented himself to build an American empire but Tim acts unimpressed so I stop talking, simply nudge him with my elbow and say, "Let's go with the Iconic Mesh Polo. In red. The ladies will love it." As we walk to the cash register, a Gap on the opposite side of the mall comes into my line of vision, the fluorescent light overhead shines brighter and my mind flashes. I remember being at a Gap with my father, him buying me a pair of jeans, and even though I was growing out of all my clothes and asked to buy some T-shirts as well, I remember him telling me no, "You have to learn the value of money." I remember thinking he was a cheap bastard.

At the cash register, the memory fades. "We'll buy this style in every color you have," I say to the cashier, a pretty girl around Tim's age, fifteen, maybe sixteen, with purple lipstick and big hoop earrings.

"Are you sure? They're like $100 each," Tim says.

"So what? Your dad's got money," I say, taking out my platinum American Express. "And they're not $100, they're $96."

"Yeah but I don't need that many."

"It's not about *need*, it's about want," I clarify.

"They're very soft," the girl with the hoop earrings says, coming back with 6 shirts.

I look over at Tim and wink.

"I like your scarf," the girl says, flirting with Tim.

Tim doesn't say anything.

"What's your name, dear?" I ask.

"Jolene."

"Jolene? Your beauty is beyond compare." I smile, but I don't think she gets my reference. "Tim, don't you think that's a pretty name?"

"Um, yeah, um, it is," Tim says, blushing.

"Timmy here has got a thing for southern girls," I make up.

"What?" Tim asks defensively.

"Is that so?" Jolene smiles lewdly.

"Here," I hand Tim my American Express. "I'm going to get a Coke," I come up with an excuse to let him be alone with her, and wait outside. But Tim walks out after several seconds and isn't smiling.

"So?" I ask.

"So what?"

"Did you get her number?"

"No."

"You know what they say?" I ask.

"No," Tim says, an edge in his voice. "What do they say?"

"The bigger the O, the bigger the…" I wink.

Tim mumbles something and walks ahead.

And I don't understand why Tim didn't ask her for her number since she was clearly into him, and as we walk through the mall, I wonder if Tim's gay, clutching the handle of the Ralph Lauren bag tighter, and then I ask myself if I could still love him if he were, and we're walking past kids throwing pennies into a defunct water fountain, out the automatic doors, into the bright sunshine, palm trees shimmering in the warm wind, when I realize, of course I would, that's my father speaking, I am not my father, I don't care if he wants to be a chickenhead, I would love him regardless, and then Tim says, "I thought we were going to GameStop."

That evening, there's a car I don't recognize parked in the driveway—a silver Nissan.

"Hey Tim, do you know who's Nissan that is?" I ask, entering his room, overhearing him and his friend, Zack, laughing.

"Yeah, that's mine," Zack says. "My dad gave it to me for my birthday."

"Oh nice," I say, glancing around the room, wondering what they were laughing about. "Did Tim tell you about the car he's getting for *his* birthday?"

"What?" Tim asks.

"No," Zack says.

"Oh well yeah, he's also getting a car." I think about what car would be cooler than a Nissan. "A, um, a Porsche," I come up with. "Yeah a Porsche 911," I add, "to be exact."

"Really?" Tim asks. "But my birthday isn't for another four months."

"Shh," I say, holding my forefinger in front of my mouth, "it's supposed to be a surprise."

Tim smiles.

"What were you boys talking about?" I ask, trying to make conversation.

"Nothing," Tim says.

"You were laughing. You weren't laughing over nothing."

"We were just talking about Zack's dad's collection."

"Oh yeah?" I ask. "What is it?"

"Just soccer memorabilia," Tim says shyly, but after a pause, he goes into it. "He has a Premier League ball that Ronaldo skyrocketed into the crowd during a free-kick, back when he was on Man-U. He also has," he starts speaking faster, sounding excited, "the ball Maradona punched into the goal against England during the 1986 World Cup, one of the most iconic moments in the history of the game. He also has a signed Platini jersey and the—"

"You boys want to see a cool collection?" I interrupt. "Come with me."

Once in my study, I turn on a switch, lighting up the glass of my Brown Kentmere China Cabinet, illuminating my impressive collection of over 150 bottles of whiskey, most of them unopened. "This here," I open the glass doors and pick up a bottle, "is Hibiki 17. The finest of Japanese whiskey. It's a blend of single malts from Suntory's two distilleries, which surprises most people because you don't taste any of the graininess common to traditional Scottish blends. A bamboo charcoal filtering step is used, which gives it a sweet and gentle flavor, before it's aged in five different cask types. This is the epitome of smooth." I pour two-fingers into my Waterford Crystal tumblers for each of them. "Speaking of 17 years, this here is Michter's 20 Year Single Barrel Kentucky Straight Bourbon. They pay special attention to their barrels once they're over 17 years old, believing that after 17 years certain whiskeys can achieve an extraordinary level of quality like no other, and those are the barrels that they select for their limited bottling, such as this one." I point to the 'Limited Release' on the bottle. "Now, the difference between bourbon and whiskey, to put it simply, is that bourbon needs to be produced in America and made from 51% corn, while whiskey does not. Bourbon also needs to be stored in new charred-oak barrels. And then there's the matter of the distillation, bourbon needs to be distilled to no more than 160 proof and entered into the barrel at 125.

This may seem unnecessarily strict but that's because in the 1800's distillers were diluting their whiskies so the Bottle of Bond Act was passed in 1897, which reinforces all these factors as laws. These codes to adhere by play a crucial role in what makes bourbon the superior spirit, if you ask me." I pour them each a glass. "So what do you boys think?"

"It tastes like monkey feet," Zack says.

"No, that's what the Laphroaig tastes like," I say dismissively. "Tim, what do you think?"

"It does kind of tastes like monkey feet," Tim laughs.

I sigh, disappointed, knowing Tim has a refined palate and would appreciate the finer aspects of bourbon and whiskey if it weren't for Zack. I look at this kid, plain, boring, ordinary, and think he's the reason my son is weird, the one to blame, since at the end of the day we are a product of our surroundings and he's constantly with him, either playing soccer or video games, making immature jokes, doing something worthless, wasting Tim's precious youth. I imagine smashing the bottle of Michter's 20 Year that I'm clutching in my hand against his stupid head, the glass shattering, splitting his forehead open, blood splattering out of the large gash, but I don't want to subject my Michter's 20 Year to that kind of atrocious abuse, so I pour myself a drink instead, and down it, quelling the urge. "I bet *your* dad doesn't have a collection like this," I say to Zack, winking at Tim.

That night, while Tim and Natalia are asleep, I'm on my computer in my study, looking up the soccer players Tim mentioned earlier—Ronaldo, Maradona, Platini— and I find myself on YouTube, watching a video of Maradona, this small, curly-haired sleazeball that the internet keeps referring to as "one of the greatest football players of all time" and "The Golden Boy," juggle what looks like a yoga ball, and then I stumble upon footage of his 1994 World Cup goal celebration against Greece, where he runs towards the camera, shouting like a strung-out madman, eyes bulging, face distorted, before apparently being disqualified for doping. And then I'm watching an hour-long BBC documentary, where I find out what Tim meant by "the ball Maradona punched into the goal," as dramatic choir music plays over the controversial images of Maradona flicking his head at the same time as he palms the ball. And I end up reading articles, browsing through YouTube videos, watching interviews, all night, eagerly wanting to see what Tim sees, to fall in love with the sport the way he has, to be able to take him to soccer practice without thinking it's a monumental waste of his time, but the truth of the matter is, as the first rays of morning light peers through the window, I am unimpressed by this coke-snorting, yoga-ball juggling, cheating foot fairy. He is not Arnold Palmer.

Driving down the I-15 in my red Honda on Friday, the signs leading to Vegas soaring overhead, my eyes fixed on the wet tarmac glistening ahead. The sun glazes the clay dunes. On the Las Vegas Daily news station: A naked man beat up a hooker in the elevator at the Luxor for stealing his wallet. Groom accused of raping woman in hotel room on wedding day. One killed after wrong-way crash on Interstate 15.

At some point, I stop at a gas station, fill up my tank, and buy a Coke. I stand on the hot concrete, in front of an electric fan, letting the air cool my sweat stains, and down the soda. The plastic bag clutched in my hands slips through my fingers and is blown away in the wind. I try chasing after it but the wind whips it a hundred feet in the air and I watch as it disappears in the bright sky like a lost balloon. I keep cruising down the seemingly endless highway, in the dry October heat, thinking about how a gallon of milk is more expensive than a gallon of gas, about the rising price of chicken wings, the classified secrets concealed behind the fortified walls of Area 51 and the mutilated green bodies they've operated on, all the nuclear and toxic waste dumped on Native American land, how many six-foot deep holes have gone undiscovered out here in the desert. And then I think about the rising sea level, the intense heat waves, the increasing wildfires, and the odds that we'll all be blasted to smithereens, and I find some strange comfort in the fact that we're all going to die one day, that everything means nothing.

I'm at the Wynn casino, playing video poker at my Jacks or Better machine. I put an unlit cigar in my mouth and fixate on the screen. A cocktail waitress brings me a free drink but I need all my wits so I stack it on the chair to my side for later. I bet $1,000 and hit the draw button. I'm dealt: 5 of spades, 7 of spades, 8 of spades, Q of spades, and Q of diamonds. The amateur video poker player would hold the pair of Qs and discard the other three cards. But what I, a seasoned video poker player, do is keep the 5, 7, 8 and Q of spades, and discard the Q of diamonds, hoping for a card of spades, which would give me a flush and a payout of 30x. I do the math: there are 13 spades in the 52-card deck, I have 4 cards of spades so there are 9 spades left out of 48 possible draws. The probability is 9/48, which gives me 18.75%. The odds look pretty good. I hit the draw button. I'm dealt 4 of spades. And just like that, with simple strategy, I win $29,000.

The key with video poker is to play slower hands so I stop for a while and stare at the people playing video poker around me, wondering if any of them are as big as whales as I am in this ocean of gambling. A man is nervously chain-smoking on the machine to my side, clouds of smoke billowing, the harsh smell nauseating me. I light the cigar dangling in my mouth, point it at him and puff bigger smoke rings in his face. He coughs, "What's your problem?" I don't say anything, simply turn back around to face my machine, and put out the cigar, in case I need to ward off more obnoxious patrons later. I place another $1,000 bet. The bright lights dim. The medley of noises drown out. People fade away. Everything goes dark. When my senses snap back into focus, all I see is the monitor screen flashing numbers. And at this moment, the anxiety-ridden intricacies of life disappear, an unearthly peacefulness possesses me, like floating in the Great Continental Divide in Iceland at night, watching green lights explode across the black sky, nothing matters, nothing except drawing the unbeatable hand. A royal flush. And similarly to Picasso with his paintbrush, De Niro in front of the camera, Arnold Palmer wielding his golf club, I become one with the machine. The King of Video Poker.

I'm sitting at a diner off of Canyon Boulevard, ravenous after staying up all night gambling, and I grab the plate of fried eggs out of the waitress' hands and devour them in two large bites, washing them down with a Coke. And I'm downing my fourth Coke when I notice a young blonde with piercing blue eyes sitting alone at a booth across from me, sipping a vanilla milkshake. She's wearing a plaid mini skirt, a tight Elmo T-shirt, glasses, her hair in pigtails, and there's something rather wholesome to her, as she wraps her voluptuous lips around the long, thin straw and sucks hard. The diner door then swings open and a breeze carries her odor over to me. She smells of lavender and rose petals and it completely overpowers the strong permeating scent of cheap coffee, pancake batter, and frying bacon. I close my eyes, sniffing, wishing I could stick my nose in her luscious hair and inhale, whiff after whiff. I imagine tearing off her clothes, squeezing her breasts, spreading her long legs, shoving my fingers in her throat, her saliva slathering them up before I slide them gently into her warm, hairless pussy, listening to her feral moan, putting my fingers back in her mouth, letting her taste how juicy and sweet and ripe she is…but I then notice her pink backpack on the table and realize she's probably still in high school, probably around fifteen, sixteen, and I force myself to snap out of it.

I look around the diner, discretely tucking my hard-on into my waistband. I pick up a ketchup bottle, trying to act normal, trying to block out the invasive thought that she could be my daughter, or Tim's friend. I remember how gross it was when my father used to check out younger girls—his eyes widening, his mouth half-open, practically foaming, like some famished animal stalking its already wounded prey—how I swore I would never become a dirty old man like him. The plate overflows with ketchup.

On Sunday I'm at a Catholic church with Natalia and Tim, nodding along to the priest's sermon, kneeling when everybody kneels, reciting the alphabet when everybody recites a prayer, and I'm only here because Natalia said it would be good for Tim if I came and I'm trying to be a better father than my father was. I try not to think that it's been a week since Arnold Palmer died.

The priest says something about a mustard seed, making me crave a BLT, and that's all I can think about for a while, and as I stare at the handsome cult leader hanging from the cross, a slit of blood dripping down his stomach, I ask myself if the Eucharist tastes like bacon since human flesh apparently tastes like pork. I look around the room, wondering if anybody here questions the absurdities of their faith, how many little boys the priest has fondled, how many people are here superstitiously, how odd it is that nobody finds it cannibalistic to consume somebody's body and drink their blood, how many people here are gay, what is the worst thing somebody standing in this room has done and how many Hail Marys for murder?

At some point in the sermon, an old couple in front of us turns around to shake our hands, saying, "Peace be with you" but I politely tell them I'm a germaphobe and shove my hands deep in my pockets. Natalia and Tim are smiling, seeming content, singing along with the choir, and I wonder if Tim really enjoys being here, or if he also just comes for Natalia, since she brings him to church every Sunday, claiming it's instrumental to instill morals in a child and that religion does so classically; and I don't disagree, I wish I were simple-minded enough to believe in something so inherently flawed. I'm surprised Tim does. The golf course was Arnold Palmer's church, just like the casino is mine. When we walk out Natalia asks me if I learned anything from the sermon. I say, "Your God doesn't love me."

"Tell Tim to pack his bags," I say to Natalia on the home line after I tried calling Tim several times from my room in Vegas but he didn't answer. "Tell Tim to pack for a father son road trip to Palm Springs. I want to leave when I get back."

"Why don't you talk to your son," Natalia says.

"Can you just tell him?"

"He doesn't want to," Natalia says.

"Palm Springs isn't that bad," I say.

"It isn't Palm Springs," Natalia says.

"Then what? What is it?"

"It's, um," Natalia pauses, choosing her words carefully, "he doesn't want to go with you."

"With me? Why not? It's because he hates me isn't it?"

"Oh don't be so dramatic," she says. "What is there for him to do in Palm Springs anyways? He's a teenager, he wants to be with his friends. At least he has some."

"What's that supposed to mean?" I ask.

Silence.

"Listen I'm going to drive over and Tim is going to stop being a spoiled shit and he will get his ass in the car and that's final."

"What's the point in forcing him to do something he doesn't want to do? You think he already hates you? This will just make him hate you even more. And your attempt at some bonding weekend will be a failure."

I hang up and pace around the empty hotel room and smash a glass against the wall but nobody comes to see what the sound was and I ask myself how far I can push the line before someone does come check, what the limit is, and when the anger subsides it's replaced with something not unlike sitting through a long losing streak and being dealt a dead man's hand. I watch the cars drive by below and wonder how many fathers are headed somewhere with their sons and then I sit down hard on the bed and call Howard to ask if *he* will go with me but some young French boy answers and I hang up.

Natalia drags me to her friend's 37th birthday party, a colossal, modern two-storied house in the desert on the outskirts of Vegas, with enough glass walls to supply Murano for the year. There's a tiki bar with paper lanterns and everybody is wearing leis and drinking tropical drinks out of plastic coconuts and Hawaiian-themed songs blare through the sound system and I'm waiting for "The Pina Colada Song" to come on but it doesn't. We're standing next to the pool, talking to a woman with a purple lei hanging from her neck who tells us her husband left her to pursue a career in stand-up comedy. A local councilman tells me that the casinos are financing the sheriff's campaign. A venture capitalist says there's no better time to invest like the present. After a while the small talk with strangers all blends into the same conversation where it shifts to them asking what I do and when I tell them I'm a high-stakes video poker player they all ask, "Like Daniel Negreanu?" and I say, "No, like Bob Dancer" but they don't know who that is and I have to explain to them that *video* poker is different than regular poker and I can tell they think less of me for not partaking in the World Series of Poker and I find it all too exhausting and when I try to hold Natalia's hand she moves hers away so I drift off and find one of the Mexican waiters carrying a food tray with deviled eggs and devour them. A man with a pink lei comes up to me and says he heard I like to gamble and shit. I tell him, "No. I just like to shit." He looks at me, confused.

The orange sun starts to descend behind the hills and Christmas lights snaked around palm trees shimmer and the pool changes color, from purple to green to red, and I stare at the water, thinking if I have to engage in any more small talk the pool will stay red cause I'll have opened my wrists into it.

I wander into the glass house, down a hallway, looking for a place to hide, open the door to a random room, and walk inside. A girl, six, maybe seven, is sitting on the floor playing with her dolls. She tells me her name is Violet, that her babysitter is in the kitchen making a PB&J, and then she asks if I'll play with her. I look around at the pink walls and white stuffed animals and pink sheets on the bed before I nod and sit next to her. She hands me a purple brush and I start brushing her long brown hair as she braids her doll and she's rather pretty for her age and smells like lilacs.

I remember the scorching summer in the San Fernando Valley before my father left, when the tap water smelled like rotten eggs and my brothers and I set up a lemonade stand in front of our lawn with cardboard we found in the dumpster. I remember my father walking up the street, pulling the biggest watermelon I had ever seen in a red wheelbarrow. He sliced it with a butcher's knife and we sat on the sticky grass and ate it. I could taste the watermelon and feel the dry air and I could smell the lilacs growing in our garden and the hot plastic from trash piling up by the curb.

At some point, a Mexican woman holding a sandwich, standing in the doorway, asks, "What are you doing?"

"Umm...nothing." I stand up. "It's just her...shampoo." I pause. "It reminded me of my daughter's."

The Mexican woman nods incredulously.

I walk out and find Natalia by the pool talking about a young boy who called her hotline and wanted to feel something and almost jumped off a roof and I don't understand why he wouldn't just cut himself instead. I hold Natalia's hand and think about the little girl with the purple brush and the billboard that says, "No Limits" and Tim and Zack giggling and the way the light changes on the red marigolds.

Sitting on the bed in my suite at the Wynn after winning $23,000, I dial 0 for room service and order some inhumane wings. Howard comes on the line, says he's sending a little something up. After we hang up, there's a knock on the door. And I'm expecting to find the bellhop with the orange vest pushing a cart with complimentary chilled champagne but when I open the door a young hot blonde stands in the doorway instead. A total Royal Flush. She's wearing a sparkling golden dress and red high-heels and has lavender eyes and short Marilyn Monroe-like hair and even has a mole above her lip that I can't stop staring at, wondering if it's part of the act.

"I'm Roxy," she says. "I hear you're the King of Video Poker."

Howard sends up Royal Flushes like a beer on the house. I used to partake, even when Natalia and I first started dating, but not since we've been married. But now that Arnold

Palmer is dead, I tell her to come in. She enters the suite and starts undressing me and I tell her I'm not really in the mood but that I could use the company and she reassures me her time is already paid for and I ask her if she wants to watch a movie instead.

"You're not gonna pull some Holden Caulfield shit now are you?" she says. "You're way too old for that."

I flick through the channels. *Cat on a Hot Tin Roof* comes on.

"I *love* Elizabeth Taylor," she says. "I've seen *all* her films."

And as she sits down next to me on the unmade bed and kicks off her high-heels, I find out her real name is Sophia, that she's a student at UNLV, that she's from The Biggest Little City in the World, and at some point during the movie, after I realize she looks like what JonBenet Ramsey would have looked like if she wasn't brutally strangled at the age of six by her older brother, she lets me go down on her until she comes and before she leaves I ask if the mole above her lip is real and she says yes and lets me touch it.

That night I am sitting with Natalia and Tim at a table in Gordon Ramsay's restaurant. I ordered plenty of steak. Tim is wearing a soccer jersey for some Spanish team that might be Barcelona and a wristband that reads "Modest Mouse." Natalia is wearing a cheetah print skirt, a black blouse and Louboutin high heels I got for her birthday last year. Tim keeps picking up his glass of water with both hands and downing it in one big gulp. The waiter has filled up his glass four times now. Natalia is chewing on the slice of lemon from her water glass. I wonder what a Modest Mouse is.

The waiter brings over the Wagyu beef I ordered for the table, and before he can even take his hand away, Tim pokes his fork into a perfectly cooked piece and, without putting it on his plate, shoves it in his mouth.

"Wagyu is an old breed of beef cattle originating in Japan," I inform Tim as I place the napkin on my lap. "They are raised in a luxurious fashion with specifically tailored diets and lifestyles."

"Cool." Tim shoves another piece of Wagyu beef in his mouth.

"Wagyu beef," I continue, trying not to get annoyed by Tim's insolence, "is a highly prized meat because it is incredibly tender and has a buttery soft flavor. The intense, fat marbling gives it this rich flavor, which melts in your mouth. It's neat to leave a piece in your mouth for a few seconds and actually let it melt." I put my first piece in my mouth for a few seconds and let it melt. "The thing about Wagyu is that you have to eat it slowly to fully appreciate the complexity of its flavors."

"Uh-huh." Tim chews as if in a hotdog eating contest.

"The cows are fed beer and massaged daily," I continue, only slightly annoyed by Tim's insolence. "When it is time to slaughter them, they are spoken to gently, given a treat and then killed suddenly and painlessly so the muscles don't have time to tense up. Interestingly, Wagyu beef has the lowest cholesterol levels of all meats, even lower than fish or chicken, and it contains oleic acid which is considered good for your heart. It's also believed to have anti-carcinogenic properties."

"It definitely melts in your mouth," Natalia says.

"Isn't it to die for?" I ask Tim. "And how cool that your dad gets all this for free?"

Tim doesn't answer.

"Tim," Natalia says. "Your father is talking to you."

"Isn't it to die for?" I repeat.

"It's good." Tim raises a slice of lemon over the Wagyu and starts squeezing.

"*Good*?" I ask. "What are you doing?" I point to the lemon.

"Zack's dad cooked steak the other night with lemon and it was really good," Tim says.

I put my hand on Tim's wrist, restraining him from squirting any more lemon. "You don't put lemon on Wagyu." I pause, exhale, and then ask again, "Isn't *this meat* to die for?"

"Are you dying or something?" Tim says, looking directly at me.

"What?" I choke on some water.

There's a long pause. Tim looks down. "Why *now*?" Tim asks when he finally speaks up, barely audible, his voice uneven. "Why are you trying all of a sudden?" Tim glances at me, but his eyes water for a moment, and he has to look back down. "You can't start caring all of a sudden...Just stop...trying...Okay? It's weird. I don't want to go to fuckin Palm Springs."

Tim gets up and walks away. I push my chair out to follow him but Natalia puts her hand on my chest and tells me to let her go instead. The waiter comes over and asks, "Is everything okay, sir?"

"No," I say.

The waiter asks if there's anything he can do.

"No," I say again.

The waiter just silently stands there and I watch Tim sit by the fountain in the distance with a distraughtness that surprises me and I think about how lucky I would have felt if my father introduced me to Wagyu beef and I don't understand what I did wrong and then I close my eyes and wonder again what a Modest Mouse is. I don't think the mice are modest in Palm Springs. The odds are not looking good.

PART II

PART II

I'm getting brunch on the Strip when I see her again, the Marilyn Monroe look-alike with lavender eyes. She waves at me. At first I turn around, thinking she's saying hi to someone else. But when I realize she's not, I wave back, the knife still in my hand. She's also sitting alone and mouths to come over so I pick up my plate and sit next to her. I ask what she's doing here and she says they have the best steak and eggs in all of Las Vegas. She brings up how fun it was to watch *Cat on a Hot Tin Roof* and we talk about old movies. At some point she says she wishes she grew up in the '60s. "Why the 60's?" I ask, but before she can answer, I add: "For the Summer of love, LSD, political mayhem, the Civil Rights Act, Vietnamese monks burning themselves in protest, the assassination of MLK and JFK, the Cuban Missile Crisis, the murder of Monroe, the moon landing, Woodstock, the Manson murders?"

"No," she says. "The first airing of Sesame Street."

After she downs her mimosa, she wipes the facetious grin off her face and mentions she was planning on seeing *Pulp Fiction* tonight at the drive-in theater, "If you want to tag along, baby." The waiter brings the check and I pick it up. "Let's go Dutch, baby." She keeps calling me baby, which makes me blush. But I insist and she says, "Fine, then I'll get the tickets tonight."

Sophia and I are sitting in my cherry-red Honda at the drive-in, a giant white screen before us. Sophia is wearing faded Levi's and a Rolling Stones T-shirt, sipping on a Cookies N' Cream milkshake. I'm chewing on some Milk Duds and as the previews roll I stare at the yellowish-orange box and remember being in tenth grade and going to the movies with Samantha Wheeler. I remember hesitating to do the fake yawn move to put my arm around her during the entire movie and accidentally hitting her when I finally tried it. I remember how she ran to the bathroom and when I asked her what was wrong she told me she just wanted some Milk Duds. I hear Sophia's bangle bracelets jingle and feel like I won't bust this time because I know better. I know to offer her my Milk Duds.

"Do you want some Milk Duds?" I hand her the box.

She smiles, takes a handful and then rests her feet above the glove box.

The movie starts and Sophia keeps talking throughout, telling me about all the moments that are references to other old-time movies, and I usually hate it when people talk over movies but I don't mind when she does it. She tells me that the minute and a half long take of Jules and Vincent walking down the corridor with the camera following them is an homage to Godard's *Alphaville* where we get a minute long take of two characters walking down the hallway of a hotel. She goes on and tells me the famous scene where Jules interrogates the guy while eating his burger is a reference to Sergio Leone's *The Good, the Bad, and the Ugly* where a character enters another's home uninvited, interrogates him, eats his food, and then shoots him dead. She tells me how Mia and Vincent's famous dance scene is an homage to Fellini's *8 ½*. When Butch encounters Vincent coming out of the bathroom, right before Butch shoots him, she tells me that the close up of pastries popping out of the toaster is a reference to Nichols' *The Graduate* where a young Dustin Hoffman delivers shocking news to his parents and then toast pops out of a toaster, which adds to the shock value.

When the credits roll Sophia claps and asks for a Q&A and I look around the rundown parking lot, at a nightcrawler with yellowing teeth rapping on windows and a group of teenage boys shattering beer bottles against cement blocks and a girl in a hoodie sitting alone in her car sobbing over a pint of Ben & Jerry's and couples making love in the backseats while the batteries burn, and in the midst of this drive-in theater, one of the last, out here in the desert, I wonder what happened to the nuclear family sipping milkshakes from plastic straws. Why aren't I here with Natalia and Tim? Hopefully, Sophia will come back to my room at the Wynn. But for now, I offer her more Milk Duds.

I'm playing video poker with Sophia at the Wynn. She's sitting at the machine next to me wearing a white strapless dress, gold hoop earrings, and cherry-red lipstick. I'm wearing gray sweatpants, a white T-shirt, and sandals with socks. Slipping her some money so she can play a few hands, I realize everybody walking past us probably assumes I'm paying her. Because why else would she be with me? But I try not to think about it and glance over at her and with the way the red, white, and blue colors from the screen light up that clean face of hers, I feel like I'm having a love affair with America. She looks like she should be on one of the advertisements that line the freeway. Her face could sell anything. Religion. Toilet stools. Microwaveable meatloaf.

Sophia says she's never played video poker before, that it looks like Galaga, and after four losing hands she calls it quits and stands behind me and watches my screen. She says she never gambles because she has shit luck, doesn't eat oysters for the same reason. She only plays roulette from time to time, but even then it's just to watch the wheel spin. I tell her video poker isn't gambling, it's pure math, and it's one of the best for players in terms of the house edge. I walk her through my thought process and the quick math I do in my head. She nods, seeming rather impressed, and then takes free drinks from the cocktail waitress and offers me one. I tell her I don't drink while I play. "C'mon have ooone drink with me," she insists. I give in.

After I've had one drink and she's had three or four and I'm up $4,000, she sits on my lap and cheers me on.

"I have to ask," Sophia says. "Why *video* poker?"

"Because I don't like people." I draw a hand.

"Kings never do." She pinches my nose.

I look around the casino and with the dazzling red chandelier and floral-carpeted floors and lavishly ornamented red and white ceilings, it has the whimsical wonder of Las Vegas, yet with the opulence of Baroque royalty. The chandelier sparkles. How is *this* not enough?

"Will you be my Queen?" I hold the pair of Queens.

That night Sophia plays a carnival game and wins a Siamese fighting fish. She gives it to me. No one has ever given me anything before. And later, Sophia comes up to my room and we order jumbo shrimp and eat in champagne-colored sheets. When I wake up the next morning there's no one next to me and the pillow smells of honeysuckle. I check my phone on the nightstand. A text from Natalia reads: "Can you pick up a box of De Cecco on your way back?" I forgot to close the curtains last night and from the bed I can see the Ferris wheel with its lights spinning in the desert like a tired roulette wheel.

"You forgot the De Cecco, didn't you?" Natalia asks when I come back home.

"You have no faith in me." I put down the plastic bag on the table, take out the box, and hand it to her. Then I pull out a Coke and take a sip, cooling me down from the heat outside.

"Marco says it's important to eat carbs before a game since carbs give you power and stamina in strenuous exercise lasting as long as a soccer game."

"Who?" I ask.

"Marco. Tim's coach." Natalia boils some water.

I wonder if Natalia is sleeping with Tim's soccer coach or if she's just being a really good mother figure. I picture Natalia and the coach talking after practice, the coach putting the whistle in his mouth and letting it sensuously dangle on his bottom lip, the laughter over having something in common when Natalia finds out he's from Italy, the plans to grab coffee later in the week, the sunlit grass complimenting his olive skin and pistachio eyes, the coach being a sucker for her silicone implants, the tension rising to its apex only to be conveniently broken by Tim approaching, heightening the desire. As long as she still packs Tim his lunch.

"Marco thinks Tim can go pro," Natalia says.

"And I *think* I can become president of the United States."

"I got him a tryout for Foggia. Only two hours from Naples."

"Great. He can visit his grandmother."

"Not Naples, Florida." She pauses. "Naples, Italy."

"Italy?"

"Marco believes Tim is at the crucial age. So I called my uncle's friend who works for Foggia's U16 and set up a tryout at the end of the month. Marco agrees we need to act now or else it'll be too late. And the level of soccer is better in Europe than it is here."

"Why doesn't he just play in college?" I ask.

"You wouldn't get it."

Tim enters the living room. He's wearing blue shorts, a blue jersey, and his cleats slung over his shoulder. His hair is disheveled, his eyelids sullen, he looks like he just woke up from a nap. He scratches his stomach and asks, "Dad, are you coming?"

"Do you *want* me to?" I ask.

"Whatever."

Natalia serves Tim, who is sitting at the counter, a bowl of penne with tomato sauce and I stand still and try to convince myself that it doesn't matter whether Tim is a foot fairy or not, all that matters is that he is my son and I support him. Not across the country, an ocean, in another continent, but here in Nevada. After Tim takes a few bites of his pasta, I tell them I'll drive and on our way to the car I catch my reflection in the window and notice I'm smiling. It isn't until we pull out of the driveway and onto the freeway and the dread of sitting out under the sun for two hours while pretending to be interested in a bunch of teenagers kicking a ball around sinks in that I realize I'm smiling because I'm proud of myself for actually doing this. Maybe Tim will recognize the effort I'm putting in and in return will decide to come to Palm Springs.

Natalia and I are watching Tim from semi-packed bleachers. Natalia cheers Tim on, and at some point when Tim tackles the opponent and the referee whips out a yellow card, Natalia stands up and shouts at the referee that the tackle was clean because he was coming down the field and she sprinkles in Italian phrases, something that sounds like, "Jew." I sense people staring at us and start to redden but the embarrassment fades away as soon as I realize they're all soccer moms clutching iced caramel macchiatos from Starbucks and wearing athleisure and sneakers as if ready to sub in for their kid at any moment. And I realize how glad I am that Natalia doesn't fall into that stereotype. She does put the interests of the family, and more importantly Tim's, ahead of her own, but she does so with style. She's wearing a tight skirt and black high heels and has makeup on. She's almost suspiciously overdressed for the occasion. Sometimes I think she's done a good job of inserting herself in this country, of letting herself be Americanized. But in this moment, as she spews Italian dialect with a real Gucci purse around her shoulder, she looks like she was plucked out from some professional stadium in

Milan and planted at this peewee field in Mesquite with-out floodlights, a domed roof to shield spectators from the sun, or Nachos.

I could go for some Nachos.

"Can you sit down, ma'am?" one of the soccer moms asks Natalia. She probably drives a Chrysler Pacifica. I'd put money on her name being Kelly.

"Can I get a Capri Sun?" I ask Kelly.

"What?" She doesn't get my joke and turns back around. Natalia does and smiles at me.

During halftime, Natalia explains that Tim has to be more selfish, that he had several opportunities to shoot but passed instead. "That's something he could learn from you," she adds.

I doze off.

At the end of the game Natalia goes up to Tim and I'm about to follow her when I get a text from Sophia asking what I'm up to. I stay back and reply, "I'm at my son's soccer game." From where I'm standing, I see Natalia talking with Marco, who looks Argentinian, maybe one-fourth Italian. The sun blinds me for a moment and when my surround-ings snap back into focus, Tim is walking over to me, wiping his forehead with his jersey. I find myself not knowing what to say to him. Good game, champ? You win some, you lose some? You should have shot when you had the chance?

"You did good," I end up saying.

"We lost," Tim says, before walking away.

Sophia texts back: "Aww you're such a good dad" with a smiley emoji.

On the car ride back Tim doesn't say anything and he looks like he just lost his entire life savings on black, his eyes sullen, his head pressed against the window as if waiting for rain to fall, for the sky to be depleted of color. Natalia explains that Tim isn't allowed to play the next game because he received two yellow cards in two consecutive games.

"Okay," I say, not seeing the big deal.

"The recruiter is coming to the next game," Natalia says in a tone that insinuates I should know what she's talking about.

"Can't the recruiter come to another game?" I ask.

"You just don't get it," Natalia says.

I pull over to the side of the road. "Then explain it to me," I say, raising my voice.

Later Natalia and I are getting fried chicken and waffles at Peggy Sue's when she tells me she lost someone from the suicide hotline, that they were calling every day for the past two weeks but then stopped calling from one day to the next, that she looked them up and found their name in the obituary. She looks like she's holding back tears as she tells me this and I wonder how she can be so sad about someone she didn't even know. And then I ask myself: Is this about the loss of human life or more so about the fact that she failed at keeping someone alive, and failure does not lend to feeling special? But as the waitress fills up our water glasses I answer my own question. Of course that's what this is about. Everyone wants to be special. Be the greatest.

D r. Sivetski's office is in a nondescript building in a strip mall. When he asks me why I'm here I tell him it's because my wife handed me a phone number and said she wanted me to talk to someone since I won't talk to her and she thinks something is wrong.

"Do *you* think something is wrong?" Dr. Sivetski asks.

"I just need to sleep," I say.

Dr. Sivetski asks about my childhood. I scoff at the cliche of it. He looks uninterested, says my last name out loud, pauses, and then asks if I'm related to the famous bank robber who was on the FBI's Ten Most Wanted list for nearly a decade in the '70s. I lie and say no.

I walk past a barber shop on my way to my car in the parking lot. I touch my beard and realize I haven't shaved in eight days, not since Arnold Palmer's death. And I don't know the last time I got a good-old-fashioned shave at the barber's shop so I enter and sit on a vintage red salon chair. The barber, a Russian man with a scraggly white beard, wraps a black cape around me and then uses a shaving brush with thick bristles to gently coat my face with foam.

"Relax," he says.

Gazing at the barber pole hanging in the corner, I remember reading that the origin dates back to the Middle Ages, when poles were given to patients to squeeze so their veins would stick out for bloodletting, that the red represents the blood, the white the bandages, but I can't remember what the blue represents. I ask the Russian barber. He says the blue symbolizes the non-oxygenated blood in the veins.

"Now *relax*," he says.

I lose myself in the spinning patriotic colors and think it must be a nationalistic homage. The Russian barber uses his thumb and first two fingers to pull my skin taut and drags the sharp blade in quick upward motions around my neck. And with the polished wood paneling and the black-and-white checkered floor and the spinning barber pole, I feel safe, like nothing bad could ever happen here. Something about this $15 shave is what Natalia would call therapeutic, far more than Dr. Sivetski's $225-an-hour office. I catch the Russian barber's reflection in the mirror. He's smiling at his work and there's something rather reassuring about his smile. He then tells me he's spent years perfecting his craft and as I pay he says it's very important that we spend our time perfecting our craft because it gives us the illusion of meaning. When I reach my car, smelling the greasy lo mein from the Chinese restaurant next door, I wonder if video poker has given me the illusion of meaning.

The Wynn stops my comps. I try finding Howard but I don't see him milling around the concierge desk or the hotel lobby or any of his usual spots and then I realize I haven't seen him in a few days. I walk slowly through the casino floor toward my machine, not letting it get to me, reassuring myself that this matter will be resolved once Howard is back.

There are always a lot of old bodies shuffling around the casino floor with walkers and oxygen tanks but there are more than usual tonight and it isn't until I notice all the black caps with the American flag that I realize it's Veteran's Night. An idea Howard implemented where veterans get comps simply because they were taught how to hold a gun and blindly follow instructions like a school of small fish. But I guess an ingenious business idea because the place is swarming, not unlike a locust infestation. And maybe some of them were heroic figures on the battlefield but I know not all of them were and handing out comps to those who weren't as if it were a participation medal is destructive to the concept of merit. I think how much my father bragged about defeating the Nazis even though he was only a Second Class Seaman, how the war created a generation of hardened men making love to their egos because they fought not for fame but for morality. I wonder when that morality shifted to my father justifying an armed bank robbery, and then walking out on his family.

The veterans block my way and I have to go all around instead of just cutting through, and so it takes twice as long to get to my machine. When I finally make it, a fat non-descript guy wearing the black cap and chomping on beef jerky is sitting in my chair.

"You're sitting in my chair," I say.

"No, I'm good," he says.

"You're sitting in my chair," I say again, louder this time.

"Oh this is *your* chair?" he asks, turning to face me. "Is your name written on it somewhere?" He looks around mockingly. "I don't see faggot written anywhere."

I stare at him for a while, clenching my fist, and I know I could sit at any other machine, that it doesn't really matter in the grand scheme of things, but I decided it mattered and so it does, and I would smash his head into the glass until thick blood streams down if it wouldn't destroy my machine in the process and then he turns back to face the screen and continues to chomp on his beef jerky and I unclench my fist. First the comps. Then the veterans. Now this asshole. I walk away. Hold those cards for another day. I drive home and meticulously polish my guns in the study for hours, wondering if my life would be any different if I had fought in a war.

Natalia and I are at the River Casino in Mesquite. The casino is small and the comps aren't worth it. We used to come here often when we first started dating. The hotel rooms are cruddy and the crinkled sheets are so stiff they can only be the result of loads of dried semen hardened over the years by hookers and prom kings. And the more "luxurious" rooms have a hot tub on a patio that guarantees a rash. The palm trees on either side look tired against the desert mountains, their fronds droopy, on the verge of dying, not unlike the casino's clientele.

Natalia uses my casino card to play the slot machines. She never wins more than a few bucks. I've tried to explain to her that the house edge for slot machines is around 10%. But she doesn't care. She enjoys the dopamine rush from all the lights and dings and spinning fruit—the award system the casino so strategically implemented. She's a sucker for it.

As I play a hand of video poker, I get a whiff of something nauseating. At first I think it's one of the cocktail waitresses but after sniffing a few times I realize it's Natalia sitting next to me. I can't tell if it's her perfume, her lipstick, some new lotion or body wash or shampoo, but it's harsh and horrendous. Like rotten fruit tossed in a blender with noxious chemicals.

"What perfume are you wearing?" I ask.

"Burberry. Do you like it? It's pomegranate and rose."

"No." I rub my temples. "It's giving me a headache."

"Oh I'm sorry," Natalia says, sniffing her wrists. "I thought it smelled nice."

"Don't wear it again," I say, relieved she's wearing this perfume here in this glorified Dave & Buster's and not at the Wynn.

The cocktail waitress tending to these money machines is old and has thin black hair and bad botoxed jowls and glued-on eyebrows the shape of McDonald's yellow arches. She looks like a highway stripper, the kind of flappy fish market that harasses you for a lap dance.

"The cocktail waitresses here look like death," I say as I watch the old stripper move gracelessly around the casino floor. "I wouldn't touch them with a ten foot pole."

"What if someone said that about you?" Natalia asks.

"I wouldn't want to be touched."

Natalia rolls her eyes.

"It isn't good here because we couldn't bring Tim." I shift in my chair, uncomfortable, looking around. "At least in Vegas there's a lot Tim can do."

"Tim hates Vegas," Natalia says. "How do you not know that?"

I won $700. "Look," I say.

"Good for you."

"That's it? Just good for *me*?"

Later at the Starbucks inside the casino, Natalia orders a medium caramel macchiato; I order a Coke.

"Can I get your casino card?" she asks.

"You don't need my casino card for this," I say. "I'm paying for your drink," I pause, giving her enough time to say thank you but she doesn't and then I add, "just like I'm paying for you."

Natalia takes out her perfume bottle and sprays her neck and wrists.

At some point back at the machines, Natalia actually ends up winning. She presses her hands together, whispers something that sounds like a prayer, then claps several times, and immediately cashes out. She smiles and waves the $20 voucher. I look at her and wonder how she can be so happy with only winning $20. She seems more pleased with her $20 win than I was with my $700 win, and I can't wrap my head around it. I begin to ask myself if I'm the problem, if maybe I should be clapping every time I win, just like Natalia, regardless of the sum. "I wouldn't be caught dead at the River," I remember Howard saying to me once over fugu, a Japanese delicacy, a poisonous puffer fish containing toxins more toxic than cyanide if not properly prepared.

What am I doing here? I should be at The Wynn. I'm too big of a fish to be here. Hopefully, they fix the mix-up with my comps soon. Natalia's wide smile reveals a red lipstick stain on her tooth.

I'm on the computer in my study when I hear a loud crash. My reflex is to clutch my gun. I keep my hand on it as I slowly make my way down the stairs. But downstairs, a pool of water covers the vinyl floor and there's shattered glass scattered everywhere. The aquarium isn't on the credenza. Tim stands there, his white sneakers soaked. And then I realize what happened. I put the gun back in my holster.

"Where's the Siamese fighting fish?" I ask, running over to Tim.

Tim doesn't say anything. He uncups his hands, revealing my Siamese fighting fish. But the fish doesn't flop around, its beautiful red tail limp.

"What the fuck did you—"

"I tried saving him," he interrupts softly.

And then I notice a soccer ball spinning by the edge of shards of glass. "What did I tell you about being a foot fairy in the house?"

"I didn't…" Tim tries but can't finish his sentence. "I didn't mean to…" he tries again. "It was an…"

Tim's eyes, red and half-closed, gaze past me, out the windows and into the street. He looks stoned, like a drugged-out zombie. Who does he think he is? That coke-snorting, cheating foot fairy? I smack him hard across the face. Tim gently places his hand over his reddening cheek, as if in shock, needing to feel the sting in order to believe it. I stare at the dead Siamese fighting fish in his open hand, once so beautiful, and I want to smack him again, this dumb kid. This little shit.

Natalia shows up with paper towels in one hand, a broom in the other. "What's wrong?" she asks Tim. She looks over at me, then back at Tim, whose glazed eyes water. "What's wrong?" she asks again. "It was an accident."

"Here," I hand Natalia my credit card. "Go to Italy. I don't care anymore."

I text Sophia that I need to get away for a weekend and ask if she'll spend the weekend with me in Coronado. She replies that she would but she can't leave for a whole weekend because that's when she makes the most money. I offer to pay her. She accepts. We stay at the grand Victorian Hotel del Coronado, which Sophia gets excited about because it's where *Some Like It Hot* was shot, even though I think it's more impressive that Nixon and Reagan stayed there.

In the morning we lounge in chaise-longues by the pool where I work on The New York Times crossword puzzle and she reads *The Stranger*. After that, we relax in the complimentary spa and after breakfast we go up to our room and order a bottle of champagne and have sex in the clean sheets, the breeze billowing the beige curtains, and in the evening we take a long walk along the beach and she collects sea glass and we eat cold ice cream and watch surfers and the sunset and the shimmering green ocean.

The first night we have dinner at the hotel's restaurant on the beach, which is packed with other wealthy, middle-aged white men, and lights are strung overhead and the palm trees looming against the violet-tinged sky seem so majestic they look fake and scattered patio heaters burn and classical music plays softly. When the server asks if my daughter would like more wine Sophia and I laugh and Sophia asks if I think we look like one of those couples where the girl has daddy issues and the guy is a dirty old man.

After a few bottles of wine she cracks jokes, "Why don't you teach prostitutes about a 17th century French philosopher?" she says, pauses, and then delivers, "Because that would be putting Descartes before the whores."

And as the night grows darker and the restaurant empties out we look up at the stars, pointing out constellations. Sophia talks about how wild it is that stargazing is like looking into the past since they're all dead. I inform her that light travels 186,000 miles per second, meaning it takes light more than 8 minutes to get from the closest star to Earth, so technically speaking, yes, we are seeing stars as they were 8 minutes ago, but that does not necessarily mean they are dead. I drunkenly tell her I see my father in the sky.

"Like in The Lion King," she says. She informs me it was based on *Hamlet*.

When she asks me what my father was like, I tell her, "There's nothing to say."

The next day, we eat breakfast on the beach and she dips buttery croissants in foamy milk, asking if I want to go scuba diving, showing me a brochure. I tell her how obsessed I became with scuba diving two years ago, how I bought all the gear—buoyancy compensators, regulators, octopuses, gauges, masks, fins, snorkels, tanks, valves, dive computers, dive compasses, accessories, dive gear bags—how I explored the Rubicon Wall in Lake Tahoe, a sheer cliff that goes down to about 1000 ft., but found the whole experience underwhelming and haven't gone since. "Well let's go for a boat ride instead," she says, writing our initials in the sand, then putting her fingers in her mouth, mimicking a gagging sound, and laughing.

We rent a boat and go for a cruise and see sea lions but the boat breaks down and Sophia laughs and I fire a flare gun, trying to remain composed, and while we wait Sophia says the clouds look like white elephants, which I find lustfully original, and she starts telling me she would have an abortion if she got pregnant and I don't know why she's talking about that but I find it reassuring and kiss her, noticing a rescue boat in the distance. And when we finally make it back to shore, I get a call from Natalia who asks how Vegas is and I say, "It's great," and at some point, before hanging up, she says, "You sound happy."

During the afternoon we go for a picnic on a secluded part of the beach but the seagulls stubbornly attack our caviar and strawberries and watermelon so we drive into town to buy Alka Seltzer but don't find any; instead we buy Mentos and slip small bits in pieces of bread and feed them to the seagulls, hoping to watch them explode into a cloud of feathers and intestines, but it doesn't work and the seagulls keep squalling. We finish our picnic back in our room and imagine what life would look like together and as she eats the watermelon, she says "You're my Dmitri," and I don't get her reference but smile anyways.

We lounge by the pool, her pretty peach-painted toes gleam in the sunlight and my eyes are in a trance and I keep gazing at them so I signal to go up to our room where she lets me suck on them while I touch myself and then we have sex on the couch and she says, still on top of me, "You're pretty good for an old white dude." And I feel like I'm nineteen again and at some point I actually think I have a penile fracture and when I go down on her and taste pennies it doesn't stop me and I keep licking, sucking, slurping, as if feasting on dollar oysters, a gimlet of viscous discharge and tangy mucus and blood, and at night we have sex in the jacuzzi, gazing at the steam rising above the water, listening to the wind caressing the palm trees and cicadas clicking and chirping somewhere off in the moonlight. It isn't until she goes down on me, when she slaps my cock against her face, which I've already told her I don't like, that I'm confronted with a question: How routine is all this? And then: Is any of this real? Or am I just another client and is she doing to me what she does to every other guy? I try not to think about how she does this for a living but as she slurps her tongue around my head, I picture a pile of unpaid bills stacked on her kitchen counter.

On Sunday, after checking-out of the hotel, we're sitting on the beach with our suitcases, trying to soak up the last bit of ocean breeze before heading to the airport. I ask if she wants to extend our stay. She says, without looking at me, gazing at brown palm fronds being washed up against the shore, "I can't, baby. I have class tomorrow."

A white car pulls up by the curb out front. Natalia and Tim wheel their suitcases out the front door, down the driveway. I walk out after them in my sandals and watch as they get ready to leave. The Uber driver, some dark-skinned Middle Eastern, the kind of guy you're glad is driving the car to get you to the airport instead of the guy sitting next to you on the plane, gets out and helps them load the suitcases into the trunk.

"Where are you traveling to on this lovely day?" the driver asks.

"Italy," Natalia says. "We're going to Naples for his soccer tryout." She pats Tim's shoulder with a certain pridefulness, as if he were her biological son.

"Wow, a soccer tryout in Italia," the driver marvels. "How wonderful."

"Yes." Natalia glances over at me. "It is quite *wonderful.*"

"And you, sir? Are you going with them?"

Before I can say anything, Natalia answers, "No, he's not."

"Dad has to work?" the driver asks. "My family stayed in my country but I work here and send money." The driver looks at Tim, then me, and says, "Maybe Dad will come later, yeah?"

Tim gets in the car without looking at me. "I'll text you when we land," Natalia says before joining Tim in the back-seat. I nod and stare at Tim through the tinted window who is clutching a backpack on his lap, wearing sunglasses, and at some point he turns his head to the side and I think he's going to raise his hand to offer a slight wave or give me a half-hearted goodbye with his wounded puppy eyes but he doesn't do either; he just turns to grab the seatbelt.

The sun shifts in the sky, casting dark shadows across the asphalt. As the white car pulls out of the cul-de-sac and recedes in the distance, leaving me alone on the side of the curb, it occurs to me that the driver doesn't think Natalia is a gold digger or Tim is a shitty son, but that I'm the guilty one in all this, that I'm the bad father.

Back inside, I sit on the couch, close my eyes, and enjoy the silence. All I hear is the white noise of the fan. That night, I lie in bed but can't sleep so I take twenty milligrams of Valium and pace the empty house, which feels a lot bigger without Natalia and Tim. Their plane must be halfway to Italy by now. I think about them soaring across the Atlantic at 500 miles per hour and wonder if they too are having trouble sleeping. I picture Tim watching some dumb superhero movie on the small TV screen, unfazed by the occasional bouts of turbulence. I don't see him pressing his forehead against the window and making peace with the fact that his life has amounted to nothing as he entertains the possibility of the plane suddenly plunging 40,000 ft down into the dark depths of the ocean. I picture Natalia flipping through *Vogue* Italia, sipping on her third glass of Merlot, snacking on complimentary almonds.

I sit by the pool and look up plane crashes, then I stare at the canvas of stars stretched out above barren land and count them. Energy can't be created nor destroyed, I remember. The balls of gas burning in the desert sky look like floating dead men. I see Arnold and Frank and Elvis and Nixon and even my father with his violet-tinted glasses and Dutch Master cigar. I don't stop counting.

When I step outside, the sun hurts my eyes, and I put on my sunglasses. The tinted lenses render everything the same shade of orange. The trees circling the cul-de-sac seem ominous. The branches sprawl like odious tarantulas. There go the Robertsons walking their dog. They wave at me. I don't wave back, I just keep staring at them, wondering how dead inside they must be to walk that creature three times a day, every day, three hundred and sixty-five days a year, every year, without fault. I get in my car, relieved it's parked in the driveway instead of the garage so I don't have to think about how long it would take for the carbon monoxide to take hold, and then I drive to a nearby Mobile and buy a box of Twinkies. I sit in my car in the empty gas station and eat the golden sponge cakes and try to remember how many days it's been since Natalia and Tim left and if that was the last time I left my house and then I think about how Howard would be a good name for a dog.

I text Sophia that I want to see her again, she replies that she's free to hang out but only if we go see some DJ named Kygo at the Encore Beach Club. I drop Howard's name to the bouncer and we skip the line. But as we enter I am already dreading that I agreed to come with her. There are people everywhere and loud music blaring and fog machines shooting clouds out into the sky. We push our way through the crowd of shirtless men fist-pumping and women in skimpy bikinis shrieking, past the DJ booth and congested bar, over to the pool.

Sophia slips her feet out of her beige sandals and dips them into the water. I look at all the disgusting-looking drunks in the pool showering themselves with beer and can't help but think about all the bacteria and filth lurking in the murky water. I notice a blood-stained band-aid floating. Sophia then takes off her black dress, revealing her white bathing suit. And with her long legs and big breasts and tan complexion and her short, blonde Monroe-like hair and her plump cherry-red lips and the golden glitters sparkling around her lavender eyes she is, without a doubt, a royal flush. A timeless blonde bombshell. And I want to get a drink but I know I can't leave her alone, that a pack of hungry wolves will surround her within seconds. So I ask her if she wants to get a drink at the bar.

"Roxy?" a guy from a table to our side shouts as we try making our way toward the bar. "Hey! Roxy!" He taps Sophia's shoulder.

"Oh hi," Sophia says, her voice changing, up three octaves. "Mark! How've you been?"

"Mark?" I ask. "Who's Mark?"

"Good," Mark says. "It's funny running into you here. I've been meaning to hit you up."

"That's so sweet," she says, flirtatiously hitting his shoulder.

"Oh Mark," I say high-pitched. "You're just the sweetest."

"Mark," Sophia turns to me, "is a client."

Mark is probably around twenty-five, thirty, he has bulging biceps, protruding pecs, washboard abs, and not a single hair follicle below his thinly, plucked eyebrows. He looks like he could be in an Equinox ad or a Calvin Klein model. I picture the lifestyle he leads: the twenty-dollar celery juice, the pre-workout shake, the two-hour workout, the post-workout shake, the protein pills, the BCAA pills, the creatine mix, the counting of every gram of protein and calorie intake on a food scale, the bucket he pukes in at his crossfit gym. It sounds exhausting. I don't know how he has time to do anything else. And I wonder how smart he would be if he dedicated all that time instead to cultivating worldly knowledge. I wonder if he knows that the word "Encore" written in golden cursive on top of the hotel, shimmering in the afternoon sun, means "again" in French and not just something you shout at the end of a concert.

"Nice to meet you," he says, shaking my hand. His hairless hand feels so smooth and slick, so well moisturized. The vivid image of his seal-like fingers slipping inside of Sophia starts to flash in my head, making me nauseous.

"I'm going to get a drink." I walk away.

After slamming six shots of whiskey at the bar, I take a deep breath, then go to the bathroom. In the bathroom, sitting on the toilet lid, blocking out the loud thumping noises and the incessant snorting outside the stall, I'm staring at my hands, wondering if they're too hairy. Maybe I should wax them. And the more I stare at them, the more I ask myself, why Sophia is with me when she could be with someone like that Calvin Klein model? On my way out of the bathroom stall, some guy dressed in black hands me a towel. He knows my hands are too hairy. He's trying to help me hide them. But he then picks up a jar with dollar bills, asks for a tip, and I understand he's just the towel boy.

I wonder if Sophia would like me if I was a towel boy instead of the King of Video Poker.

I find Sophia back by the pool, sitting on the edge, her legs dangling in the water, a Ruby Grapefruit White Claw in one hand, a half-burnt cigarette in the other. She's surprisingly alone. A wave of relief washes over me. I sit down next to her and put my legs in the water. Overhearing bits and pieces of the conversations around us: "Ass or tits?" "Doggystyle." And in the midst of all this, Sophia tells me about the last time she was in love and that she doesn't want to get hurt again. I tell her I'll never hurt her. She kisses my hand.

"I don't want you seeing Mark anymore," I say. "I'll double whatever he pays."

Sophia complains that all we do is spend time in bed so we're at the Freakling Brothers Gates of Hell, an R-rated, interactive haunted house at the Grand Canyon shopping center. We're each given a waiver to sign and are told the safe word is "purgatory" and I start reading the fine print, wanting to know what I'm getting myself into, but she signs hers without even glancing at it, signs mine, and then we enter a gate with three huge glowing "6" imprinted on it and find ourselves in a dark room, eerie cries echoing. Blue lights flash on either side of the floor, outlining a pathway. We wander down it. And at some point there's a man in a Revolutionary War outfit, he's wearing a blue coat, a white waistcoat, buff facings with white linings and buttons, and he isn't holding a Brown Bess Musket but an Allen & Wheelock Drop Breech Single-Shot Rifle, which came out in 1860 when the war ended in 1783, and this anachronism irritates me and it's all I'm thinking about while Sophia squeezes my hand as we walk through a dimly-lit hall of disfigured clowns, bloody zombies and possessed nuns. And it isn't until later, when some guy in an orange jumpsuit, covered in blood, jumps out of nowhere and puts a gun to my head that I stop thinking about it, and for a second I forget the gun is fake, and close my eyes, waiting for the adrenaline rush to kick in, to feel alive, but nothing comes, I feel nothing. I look over at Sophia, who looks terrified—eyes bulging, nostrils flaring—and I keep staring at her until it's over. On our way out, I tell her about the Revolutionary War anachronism and then we drive to my suite at the Wynn.

At some point in the middle of the night, I wake up to the noise of helicopter blades whirring and I get up and walk over to the window where I watch cop cars speed after a black Escalade down the Strip, up the turnpike, along the highway, red and blue lights flashing, the helicopter swooping overhead, and I can't help but think about my father's car chase after he robbed a bank all those years ago, how special he must have felt, like he was the hero at the center of his own movie.

After the chase disappears out of my line of vision, I grab a bottle of whiskey from the mini fridge, take a few swigs, and stare out the window at the palm trees below rustling in the night, thinking I could outrun them, like father like son. And when Sophia tells me to come back to bed, I ask, without looking at her, my voice shaking, "Does having a bad thought make you a bad person?"

"We all have bad thoughts," she says. "As long as you don't act upon them."

In the morning, Sophia and I are lying in bed watching *The Good, the Bad, and the Ugly* on TV when Sophia says she doesn't like guns. This catches me off-guard so I pry and she tells me, glancing at the rumpled sheets, that her father killed himself with one, that she was the one who found the body, his brains splattered all over his desk, that it "looked like spaghetti."

I think about ordering carbonara for breakfast.

She then asks why I carry a gun. I tell her it's like insurance: "You hope you never need it, but if you ever do, you'll be glad to have it." Later, in the big marble tub, the warm jets massaging our backs, I'm rubbing Sophia's feet while she tells me her dream is to move to New York City and become a novelist, which I find surprising because for some reason I thought she wanted to move to LA to become an actress. She tells me she wants to write something that will have an impact on the world, change somebody's life, make a difference, the way *Play It as It Lays* did for her. I reach for the glass of wine on the ledge and take a sip.

"What are your dreams?" she asks.

"I don't know," I say. "When I was a kid I was at a golf course with my father and Arnold Palmer was there and things were good," I pause. "But now that feels like a dream."

"Isn't it pretty to think so?" she says in a voice that doesn't sound like her own.

After Sophia leaves, the hotel room feels empty and I walk down the deserted hall, my sandals clattering against the marble, and take the elevator to the lobby packed with guys in Acapulco shirts and wander around.

The change of temperature from the cool air-conditioned casino to the hot arid air provides a sense of shock that I find soothing and I keep going in and out of casinos all along the

Strip until I end up on Fremont. The Island of Misfit Toys for adults, a place where all the drifting misfits and outcasts and weirdos of the world have somehow come together and turned the status quo spinning madly on its head so that within this stretch of land out here in the desert, among all the neon signs and glittering lights, you become the weird one for not walking around in nothing but a diaper or carrying a piece of cardboard that reads: "Kick me in the nuts for $20" or having a leather fetish in the scorching weather. I stop and watch a street performer, some magician with a top hat putting a red ball under a cup. And as I stand in the crowd trying to discover the trick to his disappearing act, I find myself thinking how I wish Sophia were here, how she would probably make some reference to *Fear and Loathing in Las Vegas*, and then I realize I've made the mistake of letting my guard down, that she is now more than just a Marilyn Monroe look-alike with lavender eyes. The magician's red ball disappears.

I get an urgent-sounding text from Sophia that reads: "Meet me at the venetian" and within seconds later I receive a second: "ASAP"

Entering The Venetian, I scan the crowd, searching for Sophia, and I end up finding her standing next to a Dior advertisement, wearing sweatpants and a hoodie, no make-up, her eyes darting, and she's shaking like a junkie going through withdrawals and before I can ask her what's wrong she grabs my arm and brings me toward the gondolas and the next thing I know we're on one of these stupid toy boats and the gondolier starts singing in a terrible Italian accent, but Sophia still isn't saying anything, her head abruptly shifting direction every other second, and on either side of the canals are endless ads—Charlize Theron burying pirate jewelry in some desert in Utah, Johnny Depp covered in golden glitter strolling naked out of a pool—and people are taking pictures of everything, even the fake sky, a blue ceiling with painted cumulus clouds, and for a brief moment I worry the water is fake and I'm relieved when I dip my hand in and realize it's not. The scent of chlorine permeating makes me nauseous, and I start to wonder why Sophia asked me to meet her here and it isn't until we're under a bridge, in the darkness, the gondolier humming louder than the water splashing out of the surrounding lion head fountains, that Sophia leans in and, opening her mouth for the first time, whispers in my ear, "I'm being followed."

I'm standing in the sun on the Stratosphere's observation deck, overlooking the shimmering Strip as the hot wind burns. The drowning silence and the height at which we're standing at, this bird's eye view, is synthetic, making everything below look like nothing—the perfectly geometrical grid, the June bug-like cars, the mound of clay for mountains, the toy palm trees—providing a sense of detachment from the city, from everything.

"I'm being followed," Sophia says. "Are you carrying your gun?"

"Only in case of an emergency."

"This *is* an emergency."

The giant mechanical arm holding people over the tower's edge creaks ominously. Feeling the need to protect her, I ask, "What's going on?"

"I'm," Sophia starts, pauses as a Mexican couple walks by. "I'm," she tries again.

"Take a deep breath." I put my hand on her shoulder, but she jumps back.

"I'm sorry," she says. "I'm sorry. I'm just startled." She takes a deep breath.

"Sophia, why are we up here?"

"So they can't hear us."

"So *who* can't hear us?"

Sophia looks around the empty observation deck, making sure the coast is clear, and then whispers, "The cartel."

The scorching sun burns my face. Sophia ends up telling me her roommate is a social worker at a halfway house, that one of the patients, a man who always wears olive-green cargo shorts, is working for a cartel in Tijuana, using the halfway house as a front to transport drugs and to run an underage sex trafficking ring. Sophia tells me the roommate found out and that the man with olive-green cargo shorts pointed a gun to her head, threatening to kill her if she told anyone. The roommate hasn't been home in three days and a man with olive-green cargo shorts was waiting for Sophia outside of UNLV and has been following her. Sophia looks out into the distance, her eyes welling up with tears, and says that a hole is probably already dug for her somewhere out there, in the sprawling, sun-eaten desert.

I'm walking Sophia to her car outside of the Stratosphere, parked illegally in a handicap spot, when she asks me if I'll tail her home to make sure nobody's following her. She takes a right on W Sahara Ave and drives slowly towards the freeway, passing empty gas stations, defunct wedding chapels, an oil refinery, constantly checking her rearview mirror, until she gets off the ramp and, unafraid to merge on the freeway, immediately drifts between all the honking cars to the left lane, cruising like a silver ship in the sun.

Sophia lives in a second floor walk-up, behind a strip mall, at Coral Palms Condominiums. She cautiously unlocks the door. When we enter her apartment, she glances around, trying to decipher if anybody was here, if anything was moved or misplaced. Everything seems to be where she left it. I've never been to her place before and I'm surprised by how small and crappy it is, given how much she charges her clients. It looks like the kind of motel room that guarantees an STD.

The door opens up into the living room, which is really just a filthy brown couch, a cracked glass coffee table, and a small kitchen with peeling yellow wallpaper and a sticky black-and-white checkered floor. No TV. No fridge. Only dirty dishes, overflowing ashtrays, empty beer bottles, shoes, and magazines scattered everywhere. And the yellow lighting flooding everything is atrocious, making it all that much worse. Sophia walks over to the window and peers through the blinds. "He's in there," she says, pointing to a black SUV idling in the parking lot. "The man with the olive-green cargo shorts."

I march downstairs, around the building, and across the parking lot, toward the black SUV in front of a Taco Bell. The sun reflects off the windshield and I can't make out the man sitting in the driver's seat but I'm ready to bang on the hood of his car and tell him to leave Sophia alone, cartel or no cartel, and I'm clutching the .357 magnum in my holster, wondering if I would be capable of killing him, if it were to come to that, but my question is left unanswered as the black SUV suddenly drives out of the parking lot, disappearing in a haze of traffic. I find myself in front of the Taco Bell, the gun no longer in my holster, pointing it straight at where the black SUV was merely seconds ago, except now a child is standing in my line of vision, a half-eaten taco falling out of his mouth. I put the gun back in its holster. Standing in the intersection of nothingness, gazing at the neon purple bell and the palm trees looming against the afternoon sky, I think, I could go for a XXL cheesy bean and rice burrito.

Later that day, I'm at my house in Mesquite, filling out the New York Times crossword puzzle, and I tell myself that the man with olive-green cargo shorts is probably just an old client of Sophia's or a jealous ex-boyfriend, anything besides the cartel. Maybe someone at the halfway house where her roommate works is actually part of the cartel but I think it's just a coincidence that someone started following Sophia around the same time. Or maybe nobody is even following her, plenty of people wear cargo shorts, that's not that remarkable. I don't even entertain the odds that Sophia is being followed by the cartel.

But then it hits me: the pool boy is Mexican. He's probably eighteen, maybe twenty, and is wearing a white T-shirt covered in dirt stains and ratty cargo shorts, scooping palm fronds out of the water with a net. I stand behind the glass doors, fixated on him, his dark skin glistening in the sun, his muscles straining, wondering if he's a part of the Tijuana cartel. But he's been my pool boy for at least a year now, Sophia's roommate just got involved a few days ago, why would someone who works for the cartel have been my pool boy for an entire year before Sophia's roommate even got involved? That doesn't make sense. I turn my attention back to the crossword puzzle. Until a thought creeps into my mind: what if that's not my pool boy? What if they got rid of him today and that's an imposter?

I slide open the glass door and walk out to the pool.

"So, Jose?" I ask the pool boy.

"Yes, sir?"

"Where in," I start to ask but then pause, thrown off by the fact that he said *Yes, sir* in perfect English, instead of *Si, senor*. "Where in Mexico are you from?" I ask.

"I'm not from Mexico," he says. "I'm from Bogota."

"Is that close to Tijuana?"

"It's approximately 3,500 miles away," he says. Then, as if reacting to the expression on my face, adds, "In Colombia."

The sun reflects off of the net's metal handle and I imagine the pool boy with his brown skin and black eyes hitting me on the head with the metallic handle, knocking me unconscious, and when I wake up, I'm in the back of his pickup truck, rocking back and forth alongside bags of mulch and dead plants, my arms and legs bound, a straw bag over my head, and after a while, when the bag is removed, we're alone in the middle of the desert, the surrounding mountains resembling sharp daggers, and the pool boy is holding a machete, dragging me across the orange sand, over to a leafless tree, ominous branches sprawling overhead, but what horrifies me isn't the machete's silver blade in the bright sun, nor is it the thought of coyotes feasting on my rotting corpse, it isn't even the fact that it's all going to end this way, an unglorified death, in my underwear, all alone out here in the desert. What horrifies me more than anything is that the pool boy, this alien with a dreadful brown face, looks nothing like me but has black eyes just like mine. The sun flashes. The pool boy smiles and continues scooping palm fronds with the net.

The next day, I'm driving up to the Wynn, handing the keys over to the valet when I notice his brown skin and gelled, porcupine-spiked hair, and I can't help but wonder if he works for the Tijuana cartel, if when I get back into my car, it'll blow up like De Niro's in Casino. I take my keys back, and for the first time since I've become a regular high-stakes video poker player here, I park my red Honda myself. When I walk through the brightly-lit resort lobby, I realize the bellhops, the concierge, the host, the servers, the cocktail waitresses, everyone who constitutes the vertebrae extending from the pelvis of Las Vegas's underbelly to the skull that is the Wynn is Mexican.

I sense their cold gaze as I make my way over to my Jacks or Better video poker machine. I refrain from placing my first bet, observing the brown-skinned aliens with black eyes moving around purposefully. And suddenly, all the bright lights and loud noises dramatize the moment, making me hyperaware of every small movement, turning otherwise innocent behavior into suspicious actions. A curvy waitress carrying a small, black tray with colorful cocktails comes up to me, asking, "Would you like a drink?" She's smiling, grinning. Her smile seems to convey: this is going to be the last drink you'll enjoy before we hack you like a chicken in the desert. I get up and leave, trying to walk casually so as to not set off any of the aliens lurking behind machines, ambling through crowds of zombies glued to slot machines and sirens tossing loaded dice, and when I exit the casino I pick up the pace and run to the parking lot. I sit in my car for a while, engine running, my hands gripping the steering wheel, staring at the Mexicans laughing near the dumpster, wearing white aprons, covered in blood. They're everywhere.

Turning off Las Vegas Boulevard I drive into the brightness of the city's outskirts and cruise around for a while to avoid any potential tailing from a black SUV. I take winding back roads past adobe-style homes and rundown pawn shops and abandoned construction sites, get on the freeway, off the freeway, circle around a block several times, and when the coast seems clear and there are no black SUV's in sight I get back on the freeway. But by then I'm stuck in bumper-to-bumper traffic because of an accident ahead. I look over at the black Buick to my right and notice the driver is Mexican. He's not part of the cartel, I tell myself. He's just Mexican. The cartel doesn't run *that* deep. There are just a lot of them out here. But then he glances over at me and I abruptly avert my gaze to the large Caesar sign erected to my left and I try counting the Ancient Roman columns in order to remain calm but my mind drifts and I'm left wondering what the odds are that there's a mutilated body wrapped in a garbage bag in his trunk and the thought distracts me enough that I almost smash into the car idling in front.

W hen I finally make it back to Mesquite I go straight to my study and pour myself a glass of whiskey, but when I raise the glass to my mouth, my hand is shaking. I have to sit down, take a deep breath. After several drinks, I realize something that erases whatever solace the alcohol initially brought on: my whiskey collection has been rearranged. Someone was here. Was it the pool boy? What were they looking for and did they think I wouldn't notice? But then, a question that makes all the previous questions sound foolish arises: What if this is a warning?

But all of a sudden, I hear the loud noise of an engine running and blades whirring, and I run over to my study and as I peer out the window, I see a black helicopter flying suspiciously low above the palm trees, circling the cul-de-sac, as if a SWAT team could jump out at any moment, and there's no news station lettering anywhere to be seen on it and it hovers around for a while, too long for it to be military training, and I try rationally thinking about other reasons a helicopter could be hovering this low above my cul-de-sac but come up blank, so I reach for my .357 magnum, knowing they're here for me, feeling my heart pounding, racing, but the helicopter doesn't land and I stare at it as it continues to hover and consider shooting but I'm smart enough to know I would be dead within seconds so I don't, and then it flies away, the palm fronds below blowing madly in the wind.

Sophia asked if I would show her how to use a gun for self-defense against the cartel in case they come for her when I'm not around so I bring her to a shooting range out in the Nevada desert. I make sure her ear muffs are on correctly and then I unzip my black duffel bag and take out several guns. I hand her a Glock 42 and tell her it was introduced in 2014, as an all-new locked-breech "slimline" with an 83 mm, 3.3 in barrel design. The single-stack magazine is unique to this model with a capacity of six rounds. It is Glock's smallest model ever made and is manufactured in the US, unlike all the others manufactured in Austria.

I stand behind her, making sure her feet are shoulder-width apart, put my arms alongside hers, and steady her grip, but she's tightening up so I move her ear muff to the side for a second and tell her to relax, that there's no recoil, it's as smooth as barrel-aged whiskey. Just point at the target. Press down halfway, then all the way. She hits the target. After she hits the target several times and gets the hang of it, I tell her I'll give her this one. A masterfully-crafted Glock 42.

I then show her my AK-47 and AR-15. She tenses up when I pull them out of the bag and I inform her about the differences in terms of cost, maintenance, reliability, ammunition, and all aspects between two of the greatest semi-automatic military rifles ever produced.

The sun burns my eyes as we walk out of the range and I put on my sunglasses and apologize for zoning out while I was shooting but she says, "I've never seen you more at peace." I load the unloaded guns into the trunk and in the car she thanks me for the Glock and says, "But I don't understand why semi-automatic rifles are legal."

"Well first off, they get a bad rap for killing so many people when in reality doctors accidentally kill over 680 people per day whereas all rifles combined, "assault" and otherwise, kill only 500 *per year*. So when people try to ban them, they're not acting to effectively reduce death or harm itself, but chasing their Moby Dick."

"But people keep dying."

"Furthermore, the Second Amendment does not *create* or *grant* a right to anything specific at all. Contrary to popular belief, it does not mention muskets, rifles, pistols or slingshots. It only establishes the duty of the government to not infringe upon the pre-existing right of the people to own almost any "arms" they choose. Now, I know that some make up all kinds of reasons why people don't "need" certain kinds of firearms. But the fact of the matter is that the Constitution has guaranteed the *right* to own these kinds of arms since the beginning. It's imperative that the government be unable to take away our arms because our country was founded on fighting against the government for freedom. Banning all assault weapons would be unconstitutional. Simple as that."

"But people keep dying."

"Guns don't kill people, people kill people. Additionally, the AR-15 is probably the most used target rifle in the US. It is widely used for bullseye rifle competition and for coyote hunting, and varmint hunting. And it is also the most common rifle used for feral hog hunting."

"But…" her voice trails off, the car bouncing down an apocalyptic dirt road, past chartreuse cactuses and the corpse of a coyote rotting in the desert sun. "*People* keep dying."

I think about telling her that she's flat out wrong but I've had a different variation of this conversation too many times to know better than to try to convince her without spoiling the mood so I turn up the radio and let The Eagles' "Desperado" fill the silence.

Sitting in my car across from the parking lot behind Sophia's apartment complex, I'm surveilling the perimeter, making sure nobody breaks into her apartment, and I'm watching the only black SUV that has a person in it, and in the darkness of the night and because the black SUV is parked beneath broken street lights I can't make out the license plate, only the faint outline of a figure through the windshield but I'm pretty sure the man gripping the steering wheel is the man with the olive green cargo shorts. I watch the black SUV for a while and down bottles of Coke and munch on munchkins and at some point my eyes get heavy and I doze off for several seconds but I snap myself out of it and crack open another Coke, the sound of the hissing bottle seeming more ominous than it should.

At dawn the black SUV's headlights flash on, and the black monstrosity of a vehicle slowly creeps out of the parking lot. I count to ten and then tail it, following it through a dry and deserted Vegas morning, the sky streaked so orange it looks like it's ablaze.

The black SUV takes a left at the intersection of E Sahara Ave and Las Vegas Boulevard and then pulls up into the vacant lot of a seedy motel. I've seen enough noir movies to know better than to tail a car that closely so I keep driving and park around the corner.

There's nothing worth noting about the motel besides that the stairs and walls and doors are all a different shade of pink, as if a flamingo ejaculated all over the place. And the L in the MOTEL sign is defunct and I think about the expression, a mote in someone's eye, as I walk cautiously toward the black SUV. For a brief moment I think about Miss Mooney and wonder if she still works at a motel.

The black SUV is parked in front of a room on the first floor and I try peeking in the windows of the car to see if I can spot a gun or anything suspicious but the windows are tinted and the windshield is covered by a silver reflector. The license plate is not out of state and reads: "890H14." But then I notice that the trunk has had a brand new coat of paint. Why just the trunk? To cover up blood stains from a deal gone south or a sloppy kidnapping? Maybe the blood of Sophia's roommate? I crouch down and slowly approach the room. The curtains are drawn but there's a small sliver that I can peer through and I'm bracing myself, clutching the gun in my holster, expecting to witness a violent murder, when I see the man with the olive-green cargo shorts. It's him. It's the same man Sophia pointed at from her apartment window.

He hands a manila envelope to a man in a suit who looks rather familiar and I recognize his elephant seal nose. Howard. But then Howard unbuckles his belt. I clench my gun tightly. And I find myself unable to look away, watching as Howard hauls the man who is no longer wearing olive-green cargo shorts onto all fours in a skeevy pink motel room in the wee small hours of the morning. When I finally look away, the Stratosphere Tower stands erect against a bright blue sky and I get back in my car, almost wishing I witnessed a murder instead.

I make plans with Howard to meet at Mizuya Sushi to confront him. I get there early and down a glass of whiskey to calm the nerves, wondering what his excuse will be for being in bed with someone who works for the cartel.

"I saw you with him," I say, as soon as Howard sits down next to me.

"Who?" Howard asks.

Suddenly Howard's elephant seal-like nose takes on an ominous tone. "The man from the cartel."

"What are you talking about?"

"The man with the olive-green cargo shorts. I know he works for the cartel. And I saw you with him."

"I don't know what you're talking about," Howard says. The waiter brings Howard over his usual—a spicy salmon roll, a dragon roll, an Alaska roll, an eel roll, and a tiger roll. "Listen," he continues, mixing some wasabi in soy sauce. "Sophia got mixed up with some pretty bad people when she first came out here. I loaned her a decent chunk of change to get her out of it and give her some breathing room. And now I hear that she is planning on moving to New York and I'm just making sure she doesn't skip town before settling her debt. Do you follow?"

"So the cartel isn't following her?" I ask Howard. "They aren't following me?"

"Um no."

"How much of a chunk of change are we talking?"

"Twenty-five grand."

"Twenty-five? That's it? She couldn't pay that back with all her clients?"

"Well Sophia has a bit of a problem, don't you know that?"

"What kind of problem?"

Howard wipes his nose with his finger.

"I'll pay it," I say.

There's a silence.

"I'm sorry about the comps," Howard says. "You know it wasn't personal, right? There was nothing I could do about it. You just became a liability to the casino is all."

There's another silence, this one longer.

"Y'know I'm thinking about entering The World Series of Poker," I say.

"Why?"

"People don't know Bob Dancer."

"Who?"

"Exactly," I say. "But they know Daniel Negreanu."

"Did you know that Daniel Negreanu is vegan?" Howard says. "Yeah, it's true. He always asks for pounds of tofu and oatmeal sent up to his room."

"I need to be the greatest at something more than video-poker if I want to be remembered."

"But why *poker*?" Howard asks in a tone suggesting poker is as distant to video-poker as underwater welding.

"Because what else are my options?" I say. "I'm too old for anything else."

"You'd be terrible at poker," Howard says. He puts more wasabi in his soy sauce, stirs it around, stares at it, and after a while, without looking at me, adds, "You're not good with people."

W hen I make it back home that night I get in bed and try to sleep but a coyote howling somewhere in the distance keeps me up. *Shut up*, I mumble. *Shut up*. I toss and turn for what feels like hours. And it becomes louder and louder until it replaces the hum of the fan and is the only thing I hear. Soon the howling sounds like moaning, cries of anguish, a plea. I use a pair of binoculars from the nightstand and look out the

window, scanning the moonlit desert. There it is, lying abandoned. I get the shotgun from my study, make my way outside, past the pool, off my property, into the sprawling desert.
Walking barefoot across the cold, powdery sand, unfazed by
the rattlesnakes and scorpions, I reach the moaning, moon-
drugged coyote, raise my gun and shoot it. A loud echo rings
out and then nothing. When I get back in bed I sleep soundly.

The red marigolds are dying in the vase in my study, the
bright red petals darkening. Fuck Tim and his soccer. I consider driving alone today to the golf club in Palm Springs.
Instead I text Sophia and ask if she'll come to Palm Springs
with me for the weekend. She tells me she'd love to but she
can't because she's on the clock. I offer to pay her for her
time. She then agrees to come. At least *she's* agreeable. She
mentions she has friends from LA who will be out there for
the weekend too and that it would be super fun if we stayed
at the same hotel. The Ace. I book us a last-minute room.
Text Sophia the confirmation. She texts back: "Pick me up
at the Wynn" followed by a kiss emoji.

Somewhere on our way to Palm Springs I watch the
car's thermometer rise to 113 degrees. My nose bleeds from

the dryness and I have to pull over to let Sophia drive, who's reading some book called *A Room with a View* and wearing a white T-shirt with the In-N-Out logo that reads "Eat-Me-Out."

It's even hotter out here than it is in Vegas.

When we get to the Ace hotel, which Sophia mentioned is super hip, we meet up with her friends in the lobby who are all around her age and look like the kind of people whose personalities are defined by their artsiness. One is holding an acoustic guitar, another has pink hair. The hotel has white walls and an angular pool shaped like the piece of a jigsaw puzzle and a vintage photo booth that doesn't work and a hip caravan bar and private planes zip by and land at the nearby airport. The hotel's design is mid-century modern with an overall minimalist style, flat planes, large windows, and changes in elevation contrasts against the surrounding desert.

As we check in, Sophia's friends talk about some art installation in Joshua Tree by an artist I've never heard of and I can already tell it's going to be a long weekend and I need to take the edge off so I ask the concierge for the casino so I can play a few hands but there's apparently no casino, which seems rather misleading given the name.

"We're all so proud of you, babe," the girl with the pink hair tells Sophia as she kisses her on both cheeks. Then, noticing the reaction on my face, says, "You didn't tell him?"

"Tell me what?" I ask.

"Then what are the flowers for?" She points to the flowers in my hand.

I don't say anything, confused.

"Sophia got accepted," the guy with the guitar says.

"To the internship at the publishing house in New York City," the girl with the pink hair says.

"Why didn't you tell me?" I ask Sophia.

"I don't even know if I'm going to go," Sophia says.

"Of course you're going to go," the girl with the pink hair says. "A cause to celebrate." She raises an open bottle of Mezcal.

As we walk past the pool, over to our rooms, I count the palm trees and then look at the flowers I'm clutching to remind myself why I'm here.

Sophia and her friends lounge on the chaise longues by the pool, sipping date shakes and talking about some trip they plan on taking, something about mixing their own coyote and glamping in Airstreams. Sophia says the art installation in Joshua Tree is made of all kinds of materials: bowling balls, broken bikes, busted toilets, transistor radios, old appliances, abandoned furniture. She says the art movement is called ready-made and was coined by Marcel Duchamps in 1916 to describe works made from manufactured objects isolated from their intended use and elevated to the status of art.

I don't care to keep listening, what I want is a ready-made *buffet*. I'm famished from the long car ride and wander around the hotel looking for the buffet but they don't have one here and then I think about the Wynn's scallops and my mouth salivates and then I wish Howard were here and when I ask Sophia if she'll come to the golf club with me she says later.

At night I join them for dinner at the hotel's restaurant but they're out of the 90 days dry-aged rib eye I was looking forward to and I'm forced to order the seafood salad instead and it looks like brain matter and Sophia isn't even sitting next to me. I'm sitting next to a German videographer and a sexually ambiguous trust fund rich kid who lives in Malibu. I haven't been back to LA in a while and I ask myself if this is what it's like now, if it's only gotten worse. At some point the German videographer, thick accent, blond, blue eyes, the kind of guy Hitler would have jerked off to, brings up that his grandfather died in WWII, and I remember my father bragging about his wartime body count, how many Krauts he killed and the fulfillment that brought. The videographer and the rich kid from Malibu talk about the disembodiment of the male gaze in modern cinema, in German. I take comfort in telling myself that my father murdered this videographer's grandfather.

I order a glass of Hibiki 17 to take the edge off but the waiter informs me they specialize in artisanal cocktails and as a result only have Maker's Mark. It isn't until the end of dinner when I hand the waiter my card and he says it's cash only and in complete embarrassment Sophia pays for me that I decide I hate Palm Springs. I wonder what Tim is doing right now; I should be here with Tim.

After dinner the moon hangs low over the cool desert and Sophia and her friends get stoned and roast marshmallows by the firepit; I drive to the golf club with the flowers in the passenger seat. The golf club is closed for a private event. I try explaining to the night watchman, a short and stocky bald man with a flashlight, that I have flowers for Arnold Palmer, that I drove five hours with them earlier in the scorching heat and then another twenty minutes over unpaved roads to get here and that the flowers will die, but he doesn't care. I add that I'll be quick, I only want to place them on the 18th hole, nobody is even golfing at the moment, I won't bother anyone, I'll be in and out, but he still doesn't care.

"Why don't you just place them here at the entrance?" the watchman proposes, clicking his flashlight.

"Did he win his last PGA Tour in epic fashion and throw his visor in the air here at the *entrance*?" I ask. I hear "Octopus's Garden" playing from the radio in his booth. "Did people lay flowers down on Strawberry Fields when John Lennon died or at the *entrance* of Central Park?" I ask.

"I'm sorry sir," he says. "I would if I could but I can't lose this job."

Did I seriously come all this way only to be rejected by this unimposing watchman who is shorter than me? I scan him from head to toe. I could take him. He isn't even six feet. I could lunge at him, smash his head against the pavement, and make a run for it.

"Come back in the morning," he says. "There's no private event tomorrow morning."

I stare at the brightly-lit golf club in the darkness, the perfectly-manicured green courses in the near distance, a lush oasis even richer in history, a time capsule where Arnold Palmer may very well still be alive, and I clutch the flowers in my hand, feeling like I'm on the precipice of greatness, of achieving the goal, so close to everything being restored and alright in the world again. "Yes," I say, "tomorrow morning." I then get back in my car and drive around the desert with the windows open for a while before returning to the Ace hotel.

The next day I'm in my car about to drive back to the golf club when Sophia gets in the passenger seat and tells me to follow her friend's white Mustang.

"Um, I'm going to the golf club," I say.

"That's fine," she says, putting on her red heart-shaped sunglasses, "just be quick, we can meet them at Joshua Tree. But we want to get there before the sun gets too hot."

The drive to the golf club is different during the day and I notice crackheads hanging around the CVS trying to use the building's awning for shade, not unlike in Vegas and I find comfort in knowing the two worlds aren't poles apart. At the golf club Sophia stays in the car and she seems annoyed, calling it a "pitstop" and reminding me to "hurry up" and as I enter with the flowers I ask myself, How does Sophia not realize this isn't just a pitstop but the entire purpose of this trip for me? And after all the anticipation, the obstacles and handicaps, I'm finally here, standing next to the 18th hole. I take a deep breath and try to take it all in, but before I can I hear honks in the distance and then Sophia is blowing up my phone and then golfers approach and the moment feels ruined and I lay down the flowers but it doesn't feel special. There's no big moment of closure. I feel nothing. And when I get back in the car I think about how stupid Sophia's sunglasses look and part of me wants to drive out into the desert and fuck her face until they fall off, until I feel something.

When we get to Joshua Tree the girl with the pink hair hands Sophia a copper cup with a brewing green drink that smells bitter. I notice all of Sophia's friends are holding copper cups as well. The girl with the pink hair drinks from her cup. Sophia drinks from hers. Sophia then hands me her copper cup and tells me to take a few sips but I'm reluctant to drink it, not knowing what it is.

"It's peyote," she says.

The guy with the acoustic guitar says, "Did you guys know Joshua trees were named after the Old Testament prophet Joshua because the branches reminded the early Mormon settlers of Joshua raising his arms to," he pauses, searching for the word, "pray?"

"You look like you could use it," Sophia says to me. "You've been tense all weekend."

I've been wandering out in the desert for two hours, or maybe it's only been two minutes. There's no shade and the heat is unbearable and my sunglasses are broken and I feel like I'm going to faint. I can somehow hear the color blue from the sky and I can see the sound of the wind and the Joshua Trees start to look like a sea of people praying. A visor hits me in the back of the head.

When I turn around I notice a shirtless old man higher up on a boulder and the skin around his chest sags and he's barefoot and wearing white pants and he's hacking away at cactuses with a golf club. At first I assume the old man is an insane nomad driven mad by the heat but then he smiles at me, and I would recognize that rugged, boyish charm anywhere.

The King.

I rub my temples. I must be painfully high to be hallucinating that Arnold Palmer is still alive and hacking away at cactuses in the desert in Palm Springs. Or maybe it's the dehydration getting to me. I reassure myself that the odds of drowning in the desert are higher than dying by dehydration. Either way, I join him up on the boulder. He grabs lizards off the cactus and swallows them whole. He then splits a cactus clean in two, blood dripping out of it, and I stare at the blood-stained cactus for a while.

"Are you alright?" Arnold Palmer asks with a smile so comforting that even though the answer is no, at this moment, I forget why that is.

I smile back. Arnold Palmer stands close enough that I could touch him if I reached out, I could hug him. Does Arnold Palmer see how similar we are, both men in the desert, raised to be Kings, the only difference being that *he* is looking back at a life well played?

"Did you get my flowers?" I ask. "I went with red, your favorite."

He smiles again, as if to say I understand what you're going through, I too know what it's like to put blood, sweat, and tears into being a good father only to be misunderstood while trying to be the best at something greater, I too know what it's like to have your world unravel around you, to be rejected and spat out whole.

"Why couldn't my father be more like you?" I ask.

There's a long silence. And I think, What brought me to this point in my life? And I think, I'm sick of oscillating between a video game monkey and a john. And I think, If Arnold Palmer was a good person and my father was a bad person and I can never be Arnold Palmer where does that leave me? And I think, I don't belong in this world anymore. And I think, Why couldn't I just have Arnold Palmer's life? And I realize I'm the Arnold Palmer of video poker but nobody cares about video poker and I wouldn't have heard of Arnold Palmer if he played video poker.

"My sunglasses," I end up saying, "well they're broken." I show him the lens that popped out of the frame. He will know how to fix them, put back the broken pieces.

"Maybe you just need a new pair," Arnold Palmer says. The sun shines on his white hair, making him look thirty years younger.

"Yes," I say. "That's what I need. A *new* one." A new plan to be the greatest. The greatest at something more than just video poker.

"Not everyone can be the greatest," Arnold Palmer says, putting his hand on my shoulder. He leans in and hugs me, but he's squeezing too tight, suffocating me, and something feels wrong. Prickly.

My blood boils with bile.

I place my hands on either side of his face, look at him full on, then jab my thumbs into his eyes, his eyelids clenching hard against my knuckles. Red tears spill out. I twist and squeeze tightly, shouting louder than his pleas of anguish, louder than anyone else in a world full of shouting people. I try to bring my thumbs all the way through to touch my fingers on the other side of his skull. I scoop the eyeballs out of their sockets, and then they're in my hand and they're slimy and gooey and they look like octopus balls. I toss them on the sand.

A blue lizard darts over and gnaws at one.

"I can be," I say. "I *will* be."

I take the golf club from a blind Arnold Palmer and whack him hard across the head. He falls to his knees, stunned, a large gash on his right temple revealing flesh and tissue. I turn my feet slightly to the left, perpendicular to the target, and swing the golf club against the side of his head, as if his neck is the tee and his head a golf ball. *Swoosh*. This time he falls flat, horizontal in a quick, sudden motion. A perfect high fade shot. He groans, writhing on the sand. I raise the golf club as high up as I can, then bring it back down on his head with full force. I hear a loud cracking sound. Blood spurts out onto me. I keep hitting him with the golf club, streams of blood spraying me, chunks of brain matter flying everywhere, and a piece gets in my mouth and when I spit it out I find myself almost slipping on a pinkish piece of flesh. My body is tiring so I stop for a second, but then I take a deep breath, tighten my grip, and smack his head again, and again, and again, losing track of how many times I've hit him, and I keep bashing his head in, and it finally crumples in on itself like a crushed can of Coke. The top half of his white pants now red. The blue lizard crawls up his chest, looking for seconds.

The desert sun hangs high. I step back and see Arnold Palmer painfully clear now, a man who went from selling paint to shaking the earth every time he hit a ball, but an American myth disillusioning everyday fools by dumping gasoline into the raging fire of their male egos, leaving them with resentment and bitterness when the flames burn out. The reason my father couldn't compete with the impossibly high standards he had for himself and ended up robbing banks. Arnold Palmer is why my father was an asshole and left, and ironically, Arnold Palmer is why *I* have been an asshole and why Tim and Natalia left; it occurs to me that we both managed simultaneously to be the tormentor and the tormented, the reason I've lost everything and everything around me has spiraled out of control, gone undone, untethered. The standard is no longer Arnold Palmer. What is the standard? There is no more standard…no code of conduct…I don't have to be a better version of my father, he had it right—the ends justify the means. The end. Fuck Arnold Palmer. Unlike him, I won't peak at Palm Springs. I will be the greatest. Everyone will know my name. The sun shines brighter than it ever has. A glowing beacon.

And I'm standing over him, this pathetic, unrecognizable figure, limp and still, reduced to nothing. Nothing besides remains. A gust of wind blows sand into his empty eye sockets. Rays of light gleam on the blood-stained golf club I'm clutching, my fingers wrapping the long metallic barrel. I scan my surroundings to make sure nobody witnessed anything. I stare down in the distance, at Sophia and her friends doing handstands, like ridiculous children.

They blend in with the Joshua Trees that look like a sea of people and I can no longer tell them apart from up here. Standing on this boulder, overlooking them, a sense of great purpose washes over me.

Doesn't matter what you're great at, as long as you're great at something

No Limits

PART III

PART II

I'm at The Ogden in downtown Vegas, a one-bedroom apartment I booked through Airbnb with a balcony overlooking Life is Beautiful. I stare out the sliding glass doors, and with the low buildings scattered around and the Stratosphere erected against mountains near the horizon and the bleached sky, the view looks like artifice, a video game. And I'm expecting to witness a car chase or a building implode, something transgressive, a consequential product of the city without consequences.

I wonder how many bodies are being buried out in the surrounding desert, how many young, bright-eyed girls are being drugged in motel rooms by Elvis impersonators, how many overweight men are being urinated on by escorts in presidential suites, how many addicts just bet away their child's college fund on red, how many gaming commissioners are turning their heads the other way, how many headline-worthy stories will never make the front page. This one will.

No Limits

I can see the festival in the distance, a crowd of approximately 45,000 people exactly 466 yards away. I take out the guns from my black suitcases and duffel bags and clip them into the tripods and adjust the scopes. I bring them out onto the balcony and scan the streets below, hot and empty in the glare. The big red neon shoe suspended over Fremont Street. Warehouses and parking lots. There is no music coming from the festival, they must be between sets. As I wait for the noise to come back, I picture blood, guts, bone fragments, brain matter. And even though I haven't fired the first shot, I can already hear spent shells smacking against the floor. I notice a lizard on the railing. My face burns from the heat.

I walk inside and drink a glass of room-temperature water to cool down, put a Pop-Tart into the toaster for later. Loud chants start up again by the festival grounds. I step back out on the balcony, make sure the coast is clear, no police cars patrolling the streets below, no helicopters soaring overhead. For a moment, I think the chants are for me. Thousands of people cheering me on and I welcome it. The palm trees stand tall and still and near. Through the scope, everything looks painfully clear. The aim is directed at the center of the crowd, a deluge of bullets. My finger on the trigger. I press halfway down. *Ding.* The Pop-Tart pops.

I'm driving through the deserted streets on my way to the freeway and I don't hear any sirens and I keep glancing at the rearview mirror, waiting to see police cars tailing behind or SWAT helicopters hovering above, but the road is empty and quiet, and I'm respecting the speed limit, and I can't help but wonder how different things would be right now if the sun's glare didn't cause me to need a glass of water, if the Pop-Tart didn't jolt me out of it. And as I take a right turn onto the freeway, I feel such a great sense of relief wash over me that I start to question why I feel this good if I *didn't* pull the trigger, maybe I did, and then I question my own reliability and I have to pull over to the side of the road and open the black case of ammo in the trunk and count them all just to be sure and then I think maybe there's some pleasure to be derived from being on the edge, maybe the act of almost doing it is enough, the world doesn't need to know that I could be the best shooter the US has ever seen, I know, and that's all that matters, and I ride the high of knowing I could have if I wanted to until I get to Mesquite and pull into Peggy Sue's. I sit at a booth and order some fried chicken and waffles and as I wait for the food the poster of Elvis stares at me. When I shake myself out of it, I notice I've been peeling the ketchup label. The itch is not gone. It now feels like a missed opportunity. A busted flush.

As I get back in my car in the parking lot of Peggy Sue's, I convince myself that it was not a missed opportunity because the plan wasn't thought out enough. There were several factors I overlooked: not enough guns, not enough ammo, no cotton gloves, no escape route…The more I think about it the more I realize how catastrophically the whole thing would have panned out and I find myself embarrassed at how half-assed that was. I would have just been another statistic. A number. It has to be done the right way in order for mine to stand out. Nobody can say it could have been better. It has to be the best. The red-and-white-checkered '50s themed dinner sign looms against the empty landscape, and the vast sprawling landscape makes me feel small, insignificant. I press down on the accelerator and almost run over a fat family I didn't notice walking across the parking lot. They yell at me and I swerve around them and as I enter the line of oncoming cars I think, I hate fat people, they take up so much room. I put on my sunglasses and catch myself chuckling in the mirror. With their egos.

The memorial for Howard is being held at a cemetery near McCarran airport. Geese roam the graves and the bleached sky is bright and the palm fronds glisten in the sun and I squint beneath my sunglasses. I don't recognize anybody here besides a few familiar faces from the Wynn and the man with the olive-green cargo shorts, and for some reason I was expecting to see Sophia, in a black dress that would accentuate her thinness and cherry-red lipstick. Some young guy with curly brown hair, a boy really, cries hysterically, and I wonder if they were lovers too. I stand back and stare at the coffin being lowered into the ground, and I notice the small American flags around and wonder why they aren't French flags instead. *Adieu, mon ami.*

I drove by the famous "Welcome to Las Vegas" sign on my way over here and past all the tourists waiting in line to take pictures in front of it, and I can't stop thinking about the word "fabulous." I think about the guys from a bachelor party doing lines of coke in the hotel lobby at noon. The Latin brothers sleeping on their 16oz steak after staying up for 72 hours straight. The fire-eaters at Cirque du Soleil who don't know they share their name with a group of pro-slavery Democrats in the Antebellum South. Criss Angel catching a bullet between his teeth. The homeless bums and Vietnam veterans living in the tunnels beneath the resorts and casinos. The young girls of Glitter Gulch being lured up to hotel rooms to see a baby tiger only to be drugged and sold. What part is meant to be fabulous? I think Howard saw the same Las Vegas, enabled it.

Dirt is thrown on the coffin. "Ashes to ashes, dust to dust," the priest says. I remember the post-college years when I worked as a letter carrier for the U.S. Postal Service when I was in my mid-twenties and wondering if any of the letters would be missed if I drove off a California cliff. I remember telling myself back then that I had only lived a quarter of my life and that it probably gets better. I wonder if Howard felt the same way and then realized in middle-age that, well, it doesn't. I picture Howard stepping out of his 24-jet jacuzzi, a bottle of vodka in hand, walking across his big, empty house, slipping into his clean white sheets, and swallowing twenty or thirty pills of OxyContin with vodka. I consider the odds that I'm the one who put him there. "You could always just off yourself," I said, but it was a joke. I picture a smile on his cold face when the maid found him several days later. Maybe he was onto something, had the right idea. Maybe he became well acquainted with nothingness out in the desert, found out that the roulette wheel never stops spinning so why bother betting on black. I guess the 24 jets weren't enough.

"How did you know Howard?" a woman in a black dress asks me.

A plane flies low over the cemetery.

We got sushi together. "Do you know what's in an Alaska roll?" I ask.

"You met in Alaska?" The woman in the black dress clutches a rosary and mumbles something about the Heavens.

I notice a bulldozer digging a grave in the distance and when I lock eyes with the driver he smirks and I get the ominous feeling that he seems to be saying, This one's for you.

Not until I'm the greatest at something grandiose, I reply with a confident look. Show the world what I'm capable of. What else is the point of existence if not to secure a place in history? I too have danced with nothingness out in the sun-bleached desert.

The priest recites a sermon. I remember my father telling me he wanted to open a church in Las Vegas. "Religion is the best scam," he had said. I don't stay until the end. People are always surprised by death but people die all the time. He's gone and there is no going back. Like my comps. That Frenchie motherfucker.

The party Sophia invites me to is on Clayton St, near UNLV's campus, only a couple blocks away from the Strip, and yet the contrast is quite jarring. This white house with its peeling paint job and crooked windows looks like the kind of place in the Valley where Traci Lords might have had her start.

I show up with a bottle of Hibiki 17 and ring the doorbell several times before some man, a kid really, opens the door and asks if I'm the delivery guy with the pizza. I glance down at the red Ralph Lauren polo I'm wearing. "I'm here with Sophia," I state sternly. He shrugs and opens the door.

As I walk in, I realize this party is not some small casual get-together with Sophia and a couple of her girlfriends, which was what I pictured. There are at least fifty people crammed in this small apartment and string lights hang on the walls and songs I don't know are playing and everybody here looks so young.

"What are you doing here?" Sophia asks, walking up to me.

"What do you mean?" I say. "You texted me to come. You said it would mean a lot?"

An expression washes over her, her eyes widen, her head bobs, like something just clicked, as if she now remembers texting me. "Oh right," she says. "Of course. I guess I must have, um, forgotten." She flicks the red solo cup she's holding. "Yeah because I'm blotto."

"I brought a bottle of…" I start to say, raising the bottle of Hibiki 17.

"Excuse me for a second," Sophia interrupts, hastily brushing past me, over to that girl with pink hair from Palm Springs. She's laughing hysterically by the kitchen counter. Sophia hits the girl in the arm and scolds her for something.

Sophia doesn't look drunk but she is acting strange and her face is reddening and during the quiet, transitional lull between songs I can hear her yell, "That's not funny."

People bump into me and I move to the side but it seems that no matter where I move people keep bumping into me. A girl says, "Wow you're tall." I then overhear a group of guys gossiping nearby, something about an uncle, and I wonder if maybe something happened with Sophia's uncle. A skinny blond kid wearing a black T-shirt that reads: "The Patriarchy Kills My Vibe" comes up to me and starts talking about a book called *Infinite Jest* and he goes on to explain how he's allowed to objectify women because he's sex-positive and a true feminist and points to his T-shirt and I can't help but wonder how many girls he's roofied tonight.

I don't know what to say so I start talking about the 2% rule in real estate, how if the monthly rent for a given property is at least 2% of the purchase price, the odds that it will be a good investment with strong cash flow are high. "How much for an eight ball?" the feminist asks. I tell him I don't have any and he looks confused, scanning me from head to toe, as if he thinks I'm joking and am about to hand him a small baggie and when I don't he disappears in the crowd.

"Listen," Sophia says, walking back toward me. "I'll meet up with you later, okay?"

I don't say anything, looking around, trying to understand why she wants me to meet up with her later after having texted me to come to this party, and it isn't until I lock eyes with the pink-haired girl laughing by the kitchen counter that I finally get it. "Do you want the Hibiki 17?"

"Just take it," Sophia says dismissively. "Save it for later, okay? I'll see you later, okay?"

I leave the cesspool creeping with jailbait and walk out into the night. The moon hangs despondently. I stand on an empty corner beside an overturned trash can and a flickering traffic light, not wanting to go back to my room at the Wynn, not wanting to drive back to Mesquite, and, not knowing where else to go, I decide to walk around aimlessly.

After a while, I find myself at the rooftop bar at the Wynn. And I replay the events that transpired at the party

Sophia invited me to, or at least the one I thought she invited me to, the feminist, the girl with the pink hair, the mention of an uncle. I text Sophia: "What was that?"

I stare at my phone. The screen's white glow puts me in a haze and I think back to my college days, the meaningless one-night stands ending with someone pretending they came, the long drives up the chaparral hills where I'd park by the edge of a cliff and get too high beneath pink and mauve streaked skies, the afternoons filled with going to the theater to watch black and white films and buying two popcorns so the woman behind the concession counter didn't think I was alone, the nights spent chugging cheap beer with people I didn't like and laughing at jokes I didn't find funny, the late nights at the library studying for calculus tests that ended up being insultingly easy.

Sophia looked like she was genuinely having fun at that party, despite the cliche of it all, the kegs, the red solo cups, the frat guys, the string lights, the bad conversation. I wonder why I was never able to look past all that when I was in college and just have a good time. Why didn't I make any friends?

The Eiffel Tower's pink floods look as fake as that pink-haired girl's dye.

I gaze out at this rooftop view overlooking the Strip, at the bright lights of a city that promises fantasies but instead makes you realize you're more alone than you ever thought, lights that don't just dance with the thought of suicide but inspire it.

I'm on my computer in my study looking up locations. Crowded places. It has to be the most crowded location so that I can be the greatest one. Times Square. Quincy Market. Disney World. Fremont. The Strip. There are large festivals and conventions in Las Vegas all the time. The Global Gaming Expo. The Consumer Electronics Show. The International Pizza Expo. But the convention center is indoors and all the big festivals like EDC are during the summer. So I consider outside Las Vegas.

I search: "Biggest open-air concert venues in USA." Then I compare the capacity of the venues.

The Hollywood Bowl: 17,500.

The Greek Theater: 5,900.

Red Rocks Amphitheater: 9,525.

Merriweather Post Pavilion: 19,319.

Jay Pritzker Pavilion: 11,000.

Jones Beach Theatre: 15,000.

Alpine Valley Music Theater: 37,000.

Gorge Amphitheater: 27,500.

At some point I even look into sports stadiums.

Fenway Park: 37,731.

Coors Field: 50,398.

Dodger Stadium: 56,000.

But after some basic research, I find out that festivals have higher capacities. So I look up festivals.

Around 100,000 attend Lollapalooza each day.

Milwaukee Summerfest: 73,000.

South by Southwest: 42,190.

There are two important factors to consider. 1) the closeness of the venue to Mesquite because traveling outside of Nevada means crossing state lines and 2) the ability to book a room overlooking the venue. That is the key. An overlooking room. As I contemplate all the different locations at my disposal, trying to anticipate potential issues, narrowing down the list, my computer screen slips into the idle screensaver mode, the monitor showcasing a beach. And that makes me wonder, What about *a beach*? I type into the search bar, "How crowded does Santa Monica Beach get?"

T he Santa Monica Pier has the highest population density per square mile of the entire beach. So I look up hotels with a room overlooking the Santa Monica Pier. I wonder if the arcade is still there. There are several hotels that appear close on the map, like you could throw a rock from their hotel window and hit a body, but after analyzing the scale I realize the only thing a rock could hit would be a palm tree in the downstairs parking lot. The scale on the bottom left corner of google maps indicates that 200 ft is 0.5 inches, and the total distance from the Shore hotel to the pier is 4.5 inches away so that means it's 1,800 ft, which translates to

600 yards. I follow the same procedure for the other hotels on the beach. The Ocean Lodge is 650 yards away. Hotel Casa del Mar 666 yards. The other hotels even further. The Shore is the closest hotel from the pier. But it's a boutique hotel only three stories high and with that lack of height and that distance I would need bipods. Several of them. A target area of 600 yards is feasible with bipods and scopes and the right calculations but the stakes are too high. Every detail needs to be impeccable, every step flawless. All the i's dotted and t's crossed in order to maximize the count. There's somewhere better out there than Santa Monica.

Back to festivals. Lollapalooza has the highest attendance number. An average of 100,000 a day. Fairmont and the Hilton are the two closest hotels to Grant Park, where Lollapalooza takes place. The map of Lollapalooza shows that the closest stage to the Fairmont Hotel is the Bud Light stage on Monroe Street. The Fairmont Hotel is approximately 800 yards away from the Bud Light stage. The closest stage to the Hilton is the Perry stage, which is only roughly 300 yards away. 300 yards makes the odds of maximizing the count sound pretty good. Google images shows pictures of high-rises and skyscrapers encasing large crowds packed together like sardines. There are no closeup pictures of festivalgoers. Nobody wearing denim cutoffs and fringe and exotic-tinted sunglasses. No faces ornamented with temporary metallic tattoos or bindis or a Native American headdress. Only a sea of sitting ducks against a navy blue sky.

300 yards.

That number keeps flashing in my head. And I start fervently clicking on the mouse, trying to book a room with a view before they sell out, my hand shaking. But then I come across a detail that derails the plan: Lollapalooza doesn't take place until the end of July, almost another year from now. My hand stops shaking. Back to the drawing board.

As I wipe sweat off my forehead, the prospect of getting away from this steady desert heat and going East with some brisk wind and sobering cool weather is rather appealing. And I could get some real pizza while I'm out there. Squishy dough turned into the perfect crust, the right balance of sweet tomato sauce and savory cheese. So maybe Fenway Park? Capacity of almost 38,000. That's not bad. I find a Marriott with rooms overlooking the stadium by only 266 yards. With that close proximity, a baseball hurled out of the stadium could smash my window. That ups the ante. But that means traveling across state lines.

The policies of traveling with a firearm: you can transport unloaded firearms in a locked hard-sided container as checked baggage—rifle cases require locks on each end—but you still have to declare the firearm and ammunition to the airline when checking in, and I don't want to be flagged.

I would have to drive. That would take at least 40 hours—I couldn't go over the speed limit since my father taught me to never do two illegal things at once because that's how you get caught. And driving through 10 states with a trunk filled with firearms would be the first illegal thing. So no broken headlight. No speeding. But even then, driving 40 hours leaves a large window of time for a cop car to pull me over for a routine check, a traffic stop, a sobriety checkpoint, out of boredom. 40 hours is a long time for something to go wrong. I wonder how long it would take to get a concealed carry permit in Utah, Colorado, Nebraska, Iowa, Illinois, Indiana, Ohio, Pennsylvania, New York, and Massachusetts.

The odds do not look good. No East Coast pizza.

"West Coast Best Coast" reads a bumper sticker above the California license plate on the car idling in front of me on the freeway. And even though the light hue of the sticker's color palette—orange, yellow, and aquamarine—seems to suggest a chillness, a hip laxness, arguing the West Coast is better because of the surf, the beaches, the palm trees, maybe even the fact that the burritos are superior because they come with fries inside, to me the sticker is a

beacon, a sign I had it right the first time around. Somewhere out here. I was too eager when I ruled it out once
Santa Monica fell through. Outside, the mountains sprawl
out on every side. And in the distant desert heat the mountains look small and hazy, mountains that start resembling
camouflage tree stands. I wonder how close the mountain
range is surrounding Coachella.

Turning left off of Las Vegas Boulevard onto Wynn
Main Gate Dr., past the long line circling the block for the
Encore Beach Club, I get another intrusive thought: What
about a pool party? That's a large crowd. And I wouldn't
have to drive all the way to a polo field in California. I
look up the Encore Beach Club's occupancy on my phone
with one hand as the other steers me mechanically up
the driveway toward the valet parking area. I accidentally
click on the wrong link and am brought to their website,
a virtual tour showing empty red cabanas and large white
cushions and a calm pool. I close the window, open a new
one, and re-type "Encore Beach Club occupancy" into the
search bar.

"Excuse me, sir" the valet says.

I look up from my phone.

"The keys, please. Sir."

I look back down at the screen.

Occupancy: 2,600. That's too small.

"What's that, sir?" the valet asks. "I can inquire about a bigger parking spot."

"Nothing." I get out and hand him the keys.

I'm making my way through the casino floor, to a video poker machine, when I come across a poster advertising some festival taking place right here in Vegas, at the Village, a 15-acre lot across the street, on November 1st. I stand there, staring at the poster, entranced by the simplicity of it—the eggshell paper, the Durango font—and not unlike Justice Potter at the obscenity trials who knew it when he saw it; I know it. This is the location. Two weeks from now. A country festival.

I walk over to the front desk. The receptionist is flipping through a magazine with long acrylic blue nails and I cough to get her attention but she doesn't look up so I cough again, louder this time, and then she glances up and asks, "How can I help you?"

"I want a room that'll overlook the country festival."

"I can get you tickets to the concert, if you'd like."

"Just a room," I say. "A room with a view of the concert."

"Umm sure." She clicks and clacks at the keyboard with her long acrylic nails. "Any junior suites on the north side of the 100 Wing will have a view. Room 12-135, 22-126, 32-135…But the windows don't open very much so you won't be able to hear the show that well." She pauses. "Will that do?"

"Yes," I say. "32," I mutter out loud, thinking the number sounds right, as if calling it before the white roulette ball lands on it.

During the rest of the day I roam the casino, distracted, unable to focus on anything else, going through the motions in my head, thinking about all the logistics, the amount of luggage that can fit in my car, potentially making back and forth trips to avoid the suspicion of pulling up with that much luggage, and I can't get myself to play more than a few hands of video poker and I can't even hold the most rudimentary conversation and it takes me longer than it should to realize the cocktail waitress lingering to my side is trying to take my order, her mouth moving but the words incomprehensible sounds, like she's speaking underwater, and in fact everything feels subdued, everything now colored by the assertion that I found the right location.

A country festival. In Vegas.

So I take the elevator up and lock myself in my room and continue the research on my phone and find out there will be over 22,000 attendees at this venue and that the lot across the street where it will take place is only 300 yards from the Wynn and I look up things like "How long does it take for a SWAT team to respond" and then the evening sun goes down and I find myself in the darkness and my stomach growls and then I move to a restaurant downstairs and devour a very large steak.

Back home, I unlock the gun locker in my study, take out my firearms, one by one, and set them on the towel-covered desk to inspect them.

There's the Smith & Wesson SW99 9mm semi-automatic pistol: the SW99 features an internal striker, as opposed to the classical external hammer. It is chambered in 9×19mm Parabellum, .40 S&W, and .45 ACP. The pistol lacks a manual safety; instead a de-cocking button is placed on the top rear section of the slide, which when actuated, places the firearm into double-action mode. It is the only make and model that has a double/single action.

Then there's the Smith & Wesson M&P9 9mm semi-automatic pistol: The pistol frame is made out of Zytel polymer reinforced with a stainless-steel chassis. The pistol comes with four removable and interchangeable grips. The slide and barrel are made of stainless steel, that after hardening is treated with a proprietary nitriding process called Melonite. The Melonite process produces a matte gray non-glare surface with a 68 Rockwell C surface hardness rating. The pistol has a low slide profile which holds the barrel axis close to the shooter's hand and makes the M&P more comfortable to shoot by reducing muzzle rise and allowing faster aim recovery in rapid shooting sequence.

The Glock 17 Gen4 9mm semi-automatic pistol: named because it was the 17th patent procured by the company, it outperformed eight different pistols from five other established manufacturers. The pistols contain a rough-textured frame, grip checkering, and interchangeable backstraps of different sizes. "Gen4" is rollmarked on the slide next to the model number to identify the fourth-generation pistols. Mechanically, fourth-generation Glock pistols are fitted with a dual recoil spring assembly to help reduce perceived recoil and increase service life expectancy.

There's the Mossberg 500 12-gauge pump action shotgun: The 500 series comprises widely varying models of hammerless repeaters, all of which share the same basic receiver and action, but differ in bore size, barrel length, choke options, magazine capacity, stock and forearm materials. The Model 500 is available in 12-gauge, 20-gauge, and .410 bore, but the 12-gauge is the most popular and has the most optional features available.

Then the FNH-FN15 AR-15: designed for competition, chambered in .223 Remington, it features an 18" match-grade, cold hammer-forged, chrome-lined barrel, a SureFire ProComp 556 muzzle brake to reduce recoil, a Timney competition trigger for a crisp break with a short reset, a Magpul grip and buttstock, and a 15-inch Samson Evolution handguard.

And the Daniel Defense DD5V1 AR-10 .308/7.62: The DD5V1 is a groundbreaking, performance-driven platform engineered from muzzle to buttstock. Incorporating over a decade of expertise from industry-leading Daniel Defense engineers and designers, the DD5V1 establishes a whole new standard in the .308 platform. With innovative features like a 4-bolt connection system utilizing a unique barrel extension, an optimized upper receiver, an improved bolt carrier group, ambidextrous controls, a configurable modular charging handle, and a cold-hammer-forged barrel, the DD5V1 although built around a traditional AR platform establishes a new tradition in 7.62 rifles. The NRA selected the Daniel Defense DD5V1 as the 2015 gun of the year.

I pick up this month's issue of *Guns & Ammo* from a large stack on the desk and flip through it to figure out what other pieces I should buy. *Guns & Ammo* is the most respected magazine dedicated to firearms. They focus on reviews on firearms, ammunition, optics, and shooting gear, but they also include historical articles, interviews from people in the industry, and technical evaluations on new products. I have been receiving their monthly publications for years now. I come across an article on the Ruger American .308 caliber bolt action rifle that piques my interest.

But my mouth is dry and I need a glass of water before I can keep reading so I put the magazine on the desk, walk downstairs, over to the sink, and pour myself a glass of room-temperature water. I imagine Natalia and Tim sitting on the couch in the living room watching a movie on TV. An action movie. An Arab pushes a button on a detonator.

There's an explosion at The Met. The SWAT team arrives on the scene within minutes.

"It takes a SWAT team anywhere between 30 minutes to 2 hours to respond," I hear myself say out loud.

"You know the randomest facts," Natalia would say, not looking at me.

Tim wouldn't say anything, he'd just turn up the volume.

And I would mutter, "No," drinking the glass of water with both hands. "Not random."

I drive to Guns & Guitars, the local gun store in Mesquite where I get my guns cleaned whenever I want it done professionally, at least once a quarter. There's a sign on the door that reads: "FREE gun safety course with the purchase of every firearm. FREE strap and picks with the purchase of every guitar." I pick out the Ruger American .308 caliber bolt action rifle, which *Guns & Ammo* described as "An American Legend," and 30 packs of ammo. I show Garry my Nevada I.D. and permit. He glances at them for a second, nods. I fill out the paperwork, he runs a quick routine background check, and then slides the bags to me across the counter. I shake his hand and say, "Have a great day" before walking out into the sun.

The liquor store's neon sign across the street catches my attention and I decide my whiskey collection could use another bottle. So I put my bags in the trunk of my car and walk over to Booze Galaxy. The place is empty and the only other person is some deadbeat high school student working the cash register. Fluorescent lights flicker above the shelves of colorful bottles. I'm standing in the dark spirits section when OutKast's "Hey Ya!" blares and I find myself softly humming along, tapping my foot. I close my eyes and picture dancing through the aisles, knocking down all the bottles from the shelves, twirling around the broken glass. I open my eyes. The song fades. I pick out a Hibiki 17.

The high school kid rings me up. "Um $622.40," he says, slowly rereading the number, as if to make sure he didn't misread the decimal point, his eyes as red as Mars. He's wearing some T-shirt with a skull on it and a shark-tooth necklace around his neck and he keeps picking the pimples gleaming on his forehead.

I hand him my card but he doesn't take it.

"I need to see some I.D. first," the high school kid says.

"Funny." I hand him my card again.

"I'm serious, man."

"I'm flattered," I say. "But I'm older than thirty-five, you don't need to I.D. people who look older than thirty-five. Why don't you go back to learning your capitals?"

"Hey, I'm just a cog in the machine, man," he says. "The owner told me to ID everyone. And you kind of look like a narc, man. I don't want to get busted."

I look him over incredulously for a moment before giving in to his stupidity and handing him my I.D. He runs his greasy fingers across the front, turns it around to inspect the back, tries bending it a little, and then holds it up to the light for a while.

"It's real," I take a deep breath, trying not to lose my patience. "I assure you."

"That's, like, exactly," he pauses, touches a pimple, "what somebody with a fake I.D. would say, man."

Once he finally gives me back my I.D. and lets me pay, I grab the bottle from the counter, point to his face and say, "Toothpaste."

In the garage back home, I grab the packs of ammunition out of the bags and put them in the gun safe—the Steelwater Heavy Duty 24, which usually goes for $1,999.99 but I got a deal on it and bought it for only $945. It holds up to 16 long guns and weighs over 450 pounds and has a heat activated expandable door seal that is designed to seal out smoke and water and expands up to 8 times its thickness in the event of a fire. Inside the safe are extra packs of hollow point and polymer tipped hollow point ammunition, as well as Tracer, Frangible Incendiary Armor Piercing and Armor Piercing Incendiary ammunition.

If Natalia were here she would ask, "Why do you need all this?"

"Because it's cheaper to buy in bulk," I would say. "Like chicken."

I compile 24 firearms: Colt M4 Carbine AR-15 .223/5.56, Noveske N4 AR-15 .223/5.56, LWRC M61C AR-15 .223/5.56, POF USA P-308 AR-10 .308/7.62, Christensen Arms CA-15 AR-15 .223, POF USA P-15 P AR-15 .223/5.56, Colt Competition AR-15 .223/5.56, Smith & Wesson 342 AirLite .38 caliber revolver, LWRC M61C AR-15 .223/5.56, FNH FM15 AR-10 .308/7.62, Daniel Defense DD5V1 AR-10 .308/7.62, FNH FN15 AR-15 .223/5.56, POF USA P15 AR-15 .223/5.56, Colt M4 Carbine AR-15 .223/5.56, Daniel Defense M4A1 AR-15 .223/5.56, LMT Def. 2000 AR-15 .223/5.56, Daniel Defense DDM4V11 AR-15 .223/5.56, Sig Sauer SIG716 AR-10 .308/7.62, Daniel Defense DD5V1 AR-10 .308/7.62, FNH FN15 AR-15 .223/5.56, Ruger American .308 caliber bolt action rifle, LMT LM308MWS AR-10 .308/7.62, Ruger SR0762 AR-10 .308/7.62, and LMT LM308MWS AR-10.

Bump stocks. I need bump stocks.

I drive to the Mesquite strip mall to see the Russian barber. I want to tell him my plan, see what he says, but when I ask for him, some kid who works there tells me he's never seen a Russian barber. So I end up going to the supermarket. After buying a shopping cart's worth of watermelons, I drive out to the desert and line them up on flesh-colored rocks and I practice shooting at the watermelons and watch as they explode and the bright pink chunks splatter everywhere and then I find an elevated area that I climb up to in order to create a simulation of a distance of 300 yards and a height of 32 floors and I play with the dial on the scope until my calculations for the bullet trajectory are on the money and I hit the watermelons.

Splat. Splat. Splat.

I pull up to the Wynn with four black suitcases and a laptop bag on what feels like the hottest day of the year. I sling the laptop bag around my back and try to ignore the sweat stains beneath my white T-shirt. A fat couple stands on the curb misting their faces with water from spray bottles. I tip the valet $5 as the bellman struggles to stack my suitcases on the luggage cart. "Careful," I tell him. The palm trees shiver in the warm wind and I walk eagerly out of the heat and into the cool air-conditioned lobby, the bellman in his orange vest pushing the cart behind me. After I check in, I tell the bellman I want to use the service elevator. He nods and leads the way, reeling the cart across the marble floor, snaking through crowds with the dexterity and steadfastness of Niki Lauda.

The elevator ride is quiet and we're only on the 10th floor and I don't want the bellman's suspicions to rise so I read his name tag for a personal touch and say, "Ernesto, why are elevator jokes so classic?" I pause. "Because they work on many levels."

The bellman laughs and when his laughter stops, he asks, "So what do you have in here that's so heavy?" He taps the top suitcase. "Bricks?"

The number displayed above the buttons changes slowly, from 15 to 16.

"An arsenal of assault rifles," I say.

The bellman looks at me, confused for a second, and then bursts into laughter. "Oh you're a funny guy, sir."

I crack a half-smile. The elevator bell dings. The doors open. The bellman pushes the cart out into the carpeted hallway, down the floor. He unloads my suitcases off the cart, gently places them in front of my room and then stands there for a moment and I stare at his orange vest and wonder where I can get a box of Twinkies before I realize he's waiting for me to tip him. I hand him $5.

"Thank you, sir," he nods. "Have a nice stay."

"You too," I say, and it's only after the words come out that I realize how stupid that sounds because he isn't staying here, he just works here. I guess not everybody can be a high-roller with comped rooms. But he's already halfway down the hall by then so I just mutter: "Thank *you*."

The refrigerator in the room has some kind of leftover Chinese food rotting in it, something with noodles and vegetables but I can't tell what it is because it's covered in mold. The smell is horrendous. It gives me a pounding headache. And it makes me want to pick up the refrigerator and hurl it out the window. Instead, I take several Advil and call the front desk and ask them to replace it. The woman on the other end of the line doesn't seem to think it's a weird request, apologizes, and says they'll send one up immediately. Several minutes later, someone comes in and replaces the rancid refrigerator with a brand new one, the glossy tag still on it. As soon as they leave, my headache dissipates, and then I sit on the bed, take off my shoes, and order room service. A double angus beef burger on brioche bun with provolone cheese and caramelized onions, a bottle of room-temperature water. But before I hang up there's a long silence and I become self-conscious he thinks I'm alone so I add a bagel with smoked salmon and cream cheese, what Sophia used to order. An order for two guests. I hang up, look around the room, stare at the black suitcases in the corner, and then text Sophia: "I need to talk to you. Please. Call me when you get this. It'll be good to hear your voice. I need someone to talk to."

Later, I'm playing video poker when some guy wearing a Harley Davidson T-shirt comes up to me and accuses me of sleeping with his girlfriend and he tries to pick a fight but I tell him he has the wrong guy. I say, "I'm just a guy waiting for a Royal Flush."

Standing in the parking lot of a Las Vegas Bass Pro Shop, I'm waiting to meet up with some man wearing a yellow bandana who goes by the name Skip. The ad I found on Backpage was between an ad that read: "Real Young Blonde: Bouncy & Bendy like Elastic! $300 for 30mins!" and "ever consider having a suggar dadddy?" Backpage is a more underground Craigslist and there have been several scandalous ties to the website that have made the headlines recently. Some woman from Texas claimed she had been sex trafficked on Backpage by a man who lured her in by posing as her friend. A Florida man was sentenced to 10 years in federal prison for buying sex with a 13-year-old girl advertised on Backpage. A teenager was allegedly forced to perform sexual acts at gunpoint and choked until she had seizures before being gangbanged. Some other girl was stabbed to death, her corpse deliberately burned. But Backpage also has good deals for auto sears, so that my semi-automatic assault rifles can fire like automatic ones. "$500 for auto sears and schematics," the ad read. I decided to go with auto sears over bump stocks.

The parking lot is empty, there isn't much around besides a couple of cars, looming palm trees, and a pole next to the shop with a large American flag whipping in the wind. A blue SUV pulls up towing a white boat. I don't worry about some man wearing a yellow bandana abducting me and forcing me into sex trafficking. What would the ad read: "Old Balding Fart with Hairy Hands," or maybe, "Middle-Aged Man as Bouncy & Bendy as Plywood?" Nobody would want to traffic me. One of the only perks of being a middle-aged man.

A man with a yellow bandana steps out of the SUV, holding a trash bag. I walk toward him and as we stand next to his SUV he opens the bag and shows me several hook-shaped metal pieces. I tell him I want 7 and hand him $3,500 in cash. He tells me we ought to exchange pleasantries for a moment to make the transaction seem like a nonchalant chat between friends. I scan him from head to toe and then bring up topics I bet he would want to discuss: Waco and Ruby Ridge and when he mentions FEMA camps I add, "FEMA after hurricane Katrina was a dry run for law enforcement and military to start kickin' down doors and confiscating guns." He nods, counts the money. "Somebody has to wake up the American public and get them to arm themselves," I continue, playing to my audience. He nods again, waves the stack of bills, and then hands me the trash bag. "Sometimes," I say, "sacrifices have to be made."

I'm sitting at a Jacks or Better machine playing video poker late at night when I win $113,000. The machine prints out a ticket with the sum written in a small font. I don't run over to the cashier cage to collect my winnings. I stay seated and remember spending afternoons at the arcade in Santa Monica when I was younger, holding a cup full of coins and playing Skee-Ball. The prizes were cheap and the tickets never got you anything other than a small plastic gumball machine or a snowglobe. But I remember the thrill of watching the yellow tickets slide out of the machine. The memory fades and I'm left staring at this piece of paper telling me I could buy all the plastic gumball machines in the world, but it doesn't bring the same thrill as the yellow tickets at the arcade in Santa Monica. I put the ticket in my pocket as if it were a grocery store receipt, scratch the back of my head, and keep playing.

Later I go to a convenience store in the lobby and pick out a cold Coke from the fridge but when I try to pay I realize I left my wallet in my room and I don't feel like walking across the entire casino floor to the elevator and going all the way up to my room, just the thought of it exhausts me, so I sink my hands deep in my pockets to make sure I don't have any stray bills or coins floating around and I find the ticket from earlier crumbled and I put it on the counter and flatten out the creases and then I hand it to the man behind the cash register and he doesn't say anything, just holds it up to the fluorescent light with a bemused look on his face and I tell him it's all for him and I don't think he processes what is happening because he doesn't say thank you but makes a phone call and as I walk out I picture the iconic "I'd Like to Buy the World a Coke" commercial from the '70s, the camera panning across faces of all colors singing from a hilltop about apple trees and honey bees and snow white turtle doves, and I take a sip and it tastes like the best Coke I've ever had. The bottle sparkles brighter than the glaring sea of flashing slot machines. That night I drive to Mesquite imagining a New York Post article with the headline: "King of Video Poker buys $113,000 Coke." I bring four more black suitcases back to my hotel room.

I'm sitting on my hotel bed eating a whole box of Twinkies and looking up if SWAT teams use explosives when the maid enters. I abruptly close my laptop.

"Oh I'm sorry. Do you need your privacy?" the maid asks.

"Um. No," I say. "Come in."

"Are you sure?" she asks. "I can come back later."

"It's fine. I was just, um," I look at the closed laptop and for a moment become self-conscious of what the maid thought I was doing. "Just come in." I clear my throat. "Just don't steal any earrings, okay?" I joke. But she doesn't seem to get the joke and pushes in her cleaning cart with translucent spray bottles and clean towels. "I want you," I pause, "to clean with only water."

"Just water?"

"Just water," I say. "I told the front desk I don't want any bleach or clorox or any of those foul-smelling products. They poison your mind."

"Umm okay," the maid says, as if it's the weirdest request she's ever heard, weirder than all the men who have probably asked her to clean topless. She looks out into the hall and slowly closes the door behind her.

She starts collecting the dirty towels in the corner and I stare at her, my gaze following her as she moves around the room from one corner to the other and bends down. She's young and is wearing an outfit the color of chocolate and the outfit isn't tight fitting and it hangs around her hips like a potato sack but going off how thin her ankles and legs are I would bet that she has a nice body under there and her black hair is pulled back in a ponytail and her face is what one would consider pretty with makeup on. As she bends down to pick up a third towel, she looks up and notices me staring at her but I don't look away, I keep my eyes fixed on hers, as if in a staring contest. She forces a smile and looks away before picking up the towel. Easy win.

"Is your family out by the pool?" she asks, shifting in her outfit, pulling down the hem above her knees, uncomfortable.

"What?"

She points to the eight large suitcases.

Does she know what's inside them? I panic for a second. My heart races. I stare at her eyes, then her mouth, her forehead, trying to read the expression on her face. She doesn't. She's just trying to make conversation, probably so that I'll tip her when she leaves. I look at her full on and say, "They're mine."

She nods incredulously. "I'm going to, um, clean the um, bathroom."

I watch her disappear into the bathroom as I finish the Twinkies but I don't like that I can't see her anymore so I follow her. The maid jumps when she sees me standing in the doorway, startled. I don't say anything, just stare at her for a while. The silence seems to make her squirm.

"Are you cold?" I finally ask.

She opens her mouth but nothing comes out.

"You're shaking," I say.

"Oh," she says, placing the spray bottle on the sink and holding her shaking hand with the other. "Yes… " her voice trembles.

I turn my head and read the temperature on the ther-mometer on the wall. "It's 77 degrees," I say.

"It's cold," she says, almost cautiously.

"I have to use the bathroom," I say.

She walks out hastily, accidentally knocking down the bottle on the sink.

When I come out of the bathroom the maid is gone. The room doesn't look any cleaner than before she arrived. I couldn't have been in there for more than a couple of minutes. There's no way she finished. She didn't even leave any clean towels. I call the front desk and ask them to send the maid back. Minutes later, there's a knock on the door and a maid enters but it's not the same maid.

I drive to a Honda dealership in East Las Vegas to trade in my cherry-red Honda for a black minivan. The dealer who helps me is a handsome Persian man named Bahman and it takes him saying it a few times for me to realize his name isn't Batman and he tries selling me an Acura NSW the color of mustard but I tell him I don't need the world to know I have a small penis and inform him I'm searching for a minivan and he explains the differences between the 2014 and 2015 Honda Odyssey and he goes on to say the ladies love the newest model, the sleek interior, and I tell him I only need it for the cargo space, that I'm already having relationship trouble, and he nods as if to convey he knows exactly what I'm in the market for and silently motions for me to come this way and he leads me through a door that resembles a storage unit and down a narrow, poorly-lit hallway, making it seem like he's bringing me to the back of his leather shop where the real leather is kept, and I follow him out to the back parking lot with minivans of all colors, shapes, and sizes.

I take a black 2015 Honda Odyssey out for a spin and as I accelerate past pedestrians walking on the side of the road, I think about how easy it would be to just turn the wheel all the way to the right and knock them down like bowling pins. When I pull up in the parking lot, he says I don't look like I like it. I tell him I'm just depressed. He puts his hand on my shoulder and his touch feels nice but it lingers for a second too long and I tense up and he clears his throat and then walks inside to draw up the paperwork. I purchase the minivan with $20,350 in cash. He smiles and hands me the keys and manila folder with the registration documents.

On my way out of the dealership, sitting in my new black 2015 Honda Odyssey, I toss the folder on the passenger seat. A sepia-tone photograph sticks out. I grab it and hold it up to the light. It's a naked picture of the Persian man posing on a shag rug, his pecs broad and resilient resembling two tortoise shells. This must be a mistake. He must have meant to give this to a lady client and mixed up the folders. I turn the photograph around. On the back is a note in black sharpie saying to call him, a phone number, his name signed on the bottom, and above it, next to the "Dear," written in cursive, my name.

Sophia hasn't been answering my texts and I try calling her but she doesn't answer my call either and I can't help but think she's ignoring me so I stop at a pay phone by an empty road out in the desert and call her from there and this time she picks up on the third ring. She seems shocked when I tell her it's me but then quickly readjusts and acts thrilled. She tells me she moved to New York City, that it's great, she has an interview with WME, a talent agency, she's already met a bunch of interesting people. "Doesn't Times Square look like The Strip?" I ask. I tell her to avoid Harlem but she tells me it isn't dangerous anymore and that it's where she's living. She tells me about a lounge she went to last night on Avenue B filled with models and a waterbed and a disco ball and vintage '70s Playboys scattered on all the tables with "big bushy pudandas." I start telling her I miss her but I hear someone else, a man's voice, cheering, and the sound of her swallowing something, probably a whiskey and soda, and she shouts over music blaring in the background, a song I make out to be "Common People," that she's at a rooftop party in Brooklyn and can't really talk. I clear my throat and try to tell her how much she's come to mean to me but she doesn't let me. She interrupts by saying she'll have another rum and coke, then she tells me she didn't own any winter clothes and had to buy a fur coat at some thrift store called the L train for $25 and got a free red hunting cap "like Holden." I forget who Holden is.

Standing at a payphone out in the Western desert, I picture the cold wintry Eastern light shining on her sweet, clean face and part of me is tempted to say that I will get in my car and drive all the way across this country with nothing but potato farms and cornfields to be with her but I know how mad that'll come across, I've accepted my fate, the balding middle-aged man with hairy hands doesn't end up with the young blonde capable of breaking the president's heart. She either poisons him and takes all his money or divorces him and takes half his money or goes to New York to reinvent herself and start an ambitious literary career. I think about how lovely it must be to be a blonde bombshell, the privilege of having everything handed to you, how easy my life would have been. Sophia has her whole life ahead of her and I envy that, for all I have is dread, dread and all that is already dead. I say nothing, inhaling, wishing I could smell her honeysuckle scent through the phone one last time, but instead I get whiffs of the rust on the dial. "I gotta go, baby," Sophia says. "I'll talk to you later." "Yeah…later," I pause. She hangs up.

"Goodbye, Sophia," I mutter into the beeping receiver, the sky burning so blue it hurts my eyes, the empty desert, an obnoxious mirror of the mind. *Later.* I repeat the word until I forget what it means and it sounds like gibberish and it unsettles me to think how everything loses meaning if you question it hard enough. I get back in my car and wait for the sky to darken.

I'm sitting in my Honda Odyssey on the first floor of the Wynn's self-park garage on my way back from Mesquite when a cop car pulls up into the spot across from me. There are plenty of other empty spots so the fact that they chose to park directly in front has me on edge. The two officers don't get out and the engine is running and it looks like they're staring directly at me.

Are they on to me? Do they know that I have 8 firearms in the four suitcases in the trunk and 16 more up in my hotel room, along with 600 rounds? Here I was thinking I was smarter than the police, that they would have no idea until it happened, but maybe I underestimated them. Maybe something tipped them off, the multiple trips back and forth between Vegas and Mesquite during odd hours of the night, the sudden spike in my firearm related purchases, the eye in the sky catching me on camera rolling a suspicious number of suitcases to my room with a different bellman each time, my questionable Google searches…Maybe the man from Back-page ratted me out. It could have been a number of things.

I clutch my .357 Magnum and get ready for a possible shootout. But all they would have to do is shine their bright headlights, blinding my vision, and charge from either side and I would be done for. The yellow garage lights take on a much more sinister tone. I hear myself breathing heavily. My right hand clutching the .357 Magnum blanches. And I'm almost half expecting to see a tumbleweed drift by. The cop car's red and blue lights suddenly flash and the car drives slowly toward me. I pull out the .357 Magnum, my finger on the trigger, and start raising it but before I point it at them they roll down their window.

"Everything okay, sir?" the officer in the driver seat asks.

"Yes," I say calmly, keeping the gun hidden in the shadows beneath the steering wheel.

"Alright then," the officer says. "Have a nice day." He nods before driving off.

I turn around, straining my neck, and see the cop car stopped by the garage's entrance. The officers step out and harass some black kid in a LeBron jersey for selling loose candy bars. I take a deep breath, put the .357 Magnum back in its holster, and then calmly roll two suitcases toward the elevator and up to the hotel lobby where nobody thinks twice.

I check into room 32-134 under Natalia's name, a connecting room to my 32-135, in order to bring in more suitcases without raising any suspicion, and to also shut off the possibility that someone else will be staying in that room on Sunday, which could be a liability.

"An ocean view," I playfully specify to the lady working the front desk.

She doesn't get my humor and says, "Umm we're in a desert, sir."

Today is Friday, I have to remind myself. The Route 91 Harvest country festival starts today but I've decided to be the closing act on Sunday. The headliner. After I check in to the connecting room, I walk over to the festival.

I'm standing on the street across from the country festival drinking a cold Coke in the morning heat. I can see people running in every direction, toward the steel barricades. They're screaming hysterically. A man stops, holds his stomach with both hands. A body on its side gushes blood. Other bodies drop like flies. Someone cries for help. Blood stains the asphalt. Brains splatter on T-shirts. People on their knees. A young girl covers her ears. A cowboy hat on the ground. The music stops. The sound of fireworks rings out on a hot Las Vegas night.

I lean against a palm tree, put on my sunglasses, and watch people show their wristbands to the security guards in front of the gates before entering the concert. And observing from this close, a hundred feet from the scene, not a single person aware of what's going to happen in only 48 hours, I feel a smug smile creep over me.

I wonder if Huberty visited the McDonalds a day or two before he went hunting for humans, if he smiled smugly as he stood in front of the cash register and ordered a Big Mac. I take a sip of my Coke and listen to the country music coming from the crowded lot, a lousy cover of "Folsom Prison Blues" that makes me want to shoot the rockabilly singer just to watch *him* die.

Standing under apocalyptic skies, feeling the hot winds and the dust swirling around me, I stare at these concert-goers with cowboy hats and beer bellies sagging over their belts dancing out of rhythm, and even though I recognize similar features of mine in some of them, the same receding hairline, the same hairy hands, the same average whiteness, there's nothing, no sense of kinship. Just watermelons. And I think about how they will struggle to grapple with the senselessness and will reckon the devil sent me, because how else could God allow such an ungodly act? But I have not come to do the devil's work; there is just me. A middle-aged white man playing out the cards he was dealt, raised in the desert by a rotten father and apples don't fall far from trees.

The manhole nearby reeks of rotten eggs. The palm trees lining the sidewalk tilt in the wind, leaning toward the Wynn. It's time to head back. The plan awaits.

As I start to walk away from the country festival, I look up at the hotels towering above and for a moment I'm unsettled by the thought that someone else will beat me to it, that I will be on the other side of it, but then I tell myself great minds do not think alike, basic minds do, and I am calm.

And I don't know if it's the Valium from earlier or the sugar high from the Twinkies I've been eating but all the different vibrant colors and symmetrical shapes and patterns that animate the casino floor suddenly fuse together and bounce off the screen of this machine, creating reflections that appear to recede into infinity, like looking into a kaleidoscope. I shut my eyes but when I reopen them the colors and shapes continue to twirl and I feel like I'm on psychedelic drugs.

I fixate on the screen and my limbs go numb and I lose sense of where my body ends and begins and then I get sucked into the machine and find myself swirling around. Green number grids and lines of code flash and playing cards rain down on either side. I hold cards, discard cards, draw new hands, all with my mind and after being flushed with Royal Flushes it becomes clear that I control the software algorithm to determine the outcome. 4,000 coin-payout after 4,000 coin-payout. Again. And again.

As I glide through the astral plane, the cards falling on either side become replaced by images of the past, the Queen of Spades shows a time I played Skee-Ball at the

Santa Monica arcade, the Ace of Diamonds the time my father and I met Arnold Palmer, the Four of Hearts the time Miss Mooney brought me to the motel pool, the Two of Clubs my father and mother slow-dancing on a California beach, and as I continue to glide deeper into this surreal realm I can no longer make out the cards, they're just place-holders, television sets playing snippets of old memories, my father teaching me how to play poker at the bingo parlor, accidentally hitting Samantha Wheeler at the movie theater, fighting with my brothers over the last glass of milk since nobody wanted the powdered milk, faces of temporary friends who ended up becoming strangers, the short list of woman I've been romantically involved with, a watermelon in a red wheelbarrow, a crispy chicken on a Thanksgiving table, African penguins at the zoo, a cream-colored Pontiac.

Then I drop thirty stories and hit the ground. It's dark and I can't see anything besides a sliver of light in the distance so I stagger toward it. A door left ajar. When I peer in I see Arnold and Frank and Elvis and Nixon and my father all sitting around a long conference table going over the blueprints of my life and laughing. I try to speak up but they don't hear me and then their faces appear in the black sky above, thirteen times the size of God, looking down on me, their laughter echoing louder and louder as if coming through a megaphone pressed up against my ear. They sound like a pack of coyotes howling in the desert night. I remember the one I shot, the spilled blood and guts.

I spend the nights playing video poker and the days lying in the cool AC with the curtains drawn and the sheets pulled up over my head and I don't see the sunlight for days and even the stimuli from the bright machines becomes too much that I have to play with my sunglasses on and I feel like a gambling vampire roaming the casino corridors and I wonder if vampires find any excitement in taking human lives or if they are cursed to be jaded for eternity and feel nothing and when I'm not playing video poker or lying in bed I stay in my room and take a few Valium and eat boxes of Twinkies and order room service and use the food service cart to set up hidden cameras and then before I know it it's Sunday.

Sunday.

I go downstairs and order two spicy salmon rolls at Mizuya Sushi for breakfast. I don't talk to anybody or look at my phone, I just stare mindlessly at the TV hanging above the sushi bar, and wonder how many condemned inmates on death row have sushi for their last meal.

"Big night?" the waiter asks, filling up my glass of water. I don't say anything, he points to the sunglasses on my face. "Tonight will be bigger," I say.

A life well played.

I point to the ice cubes in my glass and ask for room-temperature water. After I finish eating I charge the bill to my room and tip the waiter in cash. I then start walking across the busy casino floor but somewhere along the way "Suspicious Minds" plays and I stop for a second, the bright lights, the sea of slot machines, the stoic dealers in their maroon vests, cards fanned on tables, the spinning roulette wheels, the watermelon jackpot, the ugly movie theater carpet, *caught in a trap I can't walk out,* I take one last look, *why can't you see, what you're doing to me,* and then keep walking over to the elevators. As the elevator doors open, a family of five steps out wearing cowboy hats, band T-shirts, and matching green wristbands. The little blonde girl locks eyes with me for a passing moment and then skips away.

I enter the elevator and press the button for the doors to close before anybody else can get in and I go up to the 32nd floor. I move down the empty hallway, over to my room. I hang the red "Do Not Disturb" sign on the door's handle before locking it behind me and then walk over to the floor-to-ceiling window and I stare at the monstrous crowd surrounding the stage down by the Strip, waiting for the sun to set, ready to count.

Acknowledgments

Infinite thanks: to Tuscany, the best de facto editor, for being there since the inception, and for without whom this book would not exist; to Charles, for the utmost support and unfaltering belief, especially when it eluded me; to my dear early readers—Andi, Charlotte, Paulina, Grace, and Al; to all the many other friends and loved ones, especially my family; to Robin Mookerjee, Binnie Kirschenbaum, Josh Fuerst, Sam Lipsyte; and of course, to Christoph Paul and Leza Cantoral at CLASH books.

About the Author

Paolo Iacovelli is a French-Italian-Colombian writer born and raised in New York City. He received his MFA from Columbia's School of the Arts. *The King of Video Poker* is his debut novel.

 @paoloadrianiacovelli

Also by CLASH Books

BAD FOUNDATIONS
Brian Allen Carr

THE MAN WHO SAW SECONDS
Alexander Boldizar

VIOLENT FACULTIES
Charlene Elsby

THE RACHEL CONDITION
Nicholas Rombles

DEATH ROW RESTAURANT
Daniel Gonzalez

DARRYL
Jackie Ess

EVERYTHING THE DARKNESS EATS
Eric LaRocca

ANYBODY HOME?
Michael J. Seidlinger

THE LOGOS
Mark de Silva

Printed in the USA
CPSIA information can be obtained
at www.ICGtesting.com
JSHW082243130624
64692JS00002B/2